at are you doing here, Matt?"

oided her eyes. He'd become good at lying, but he never could to her. "I told you—I wanted to bring you dinner."

Liar. "Is that the only reason you're here?" she pressed. "To make sure I eat?"

This time he did raise his eyes to hers. "That, and because I still like looking at you, Natalie. You are still one of the most beautiful creatures God ever created."

Wow…he sure did know how to press her buttons.

"I can't do this," she told him suddenly.

"Do what?"

"I can't sit here opposite you and pretend I don't feel anything, that I don't still—"

He didn't let her finish.

Pushing his chair back, Matt was on his feet, sinking his hands into her hair, tilting her face up to his. Immobilizing her lips by feverishly pressing his own against them in a kiss that set her body on fire.

Dear Reader,

I love beginnings, when anything can happen. The beginning of a series is like that, like watching a rosebud open up and become a lovely flower. So here we are, you and I, at the beginning of LOVE IN 60 SECONDS. This series is set in Las Vegas, a city of glamour, of glitz, where fortunes and reputations are won—and lost—not only at the turn of a card, but at the whimsical hands of fate. At the core of this series are the Rothchild family and a legendary, rare diamond—the Tears of Quetzal—that is worth millions. The true, rightful ownership of the gem is in question, which leads us to our mystery. Was powerful casino mogul Harold Rothchild's daughter Candace murdered for the diamond—or for revenge?

This is the question that haunts Detective Natalie Rothchild, Candace's far more grounded twin sister. As she struggles to put the pieces of the puzzle together, Natalie finds that she has to rely on the help of a newly resurfaced Matt Shaffer, himself a member of a family with shady connections, and the man who, eight years ago, abandoned her while in possession of her heart.

I hope you find this tale of lost and found as intriguing as I did and that you'll come back for the next installment. As ever, I thank you for reading and I wish you love.

Marie Ferrarella

MARIE FERRARELLA

The Heiress's 2-Week Affair

Silhouette®

Romantic

SUSPENSE

Special thanks and acknowledgment to Marie Ferrarella for her contribution to the Love in 60 Seconds miniseries.

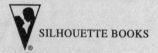

SILHOUETTE BOOKS

ISBN-13: 978-0-373-27626-4
ISBN-10:   0-373-27626-5

Recycling programs
for this product may
not exist in your area.

THE HEIRESS'S 2-WEEK AFFAIR

Visit Silhouette Books at www.eHarlequin.com

Printed in U.S.A.

MARIE FERRARELLA

This *USA TODAY* bestselling and RITA® Award-winning author has written more than one hundred and fifty books for Silhouette, some under the name Marie Nicole. Her romances are beloved by fans worldwide. Visit her Web site at www.marieferrarella.com.

To
Shana Smith.
Welcome
aboard.

Prologue

The burst of joy that bathed over her like warm summer rain when Natalie Rothchild opened her eyes began to recede as the reality of the situation slowly penetrated her consciousness.

The spot beside her on the bed was empty.

Empty and cool to the touch when she ran her fingers over it.

"Matt?" She called out his name, but only the echo of her voice answered her. There was no sound of running water from the bathroom, no indication that there was anyone else in the hotel room but her.

Her heart began hammering hard, so hard that it physically hurt her. It felt as if someone had shot arrows through it.

He couldn't have gone.

But if he was here, where were his clothes? The ones

that he'd torn off so carelessly last night, throwing them on the floor along with hers? The first time they'd made love last night, she'd all but caught on fire.

The ache within her chest grew.

"Matt?" she called out again. Fear and bewilderment filled her voice as she sat up. A chill ran down her spine. Something was wrong.

Last night, he'd told her that he loved her, told her that they'd be together forever. He'd said he wanted to marry her. She *knew* he'd meant it. Knew it wasn't just something expedient to say because he wanted to make love to her. He'd said it after, not before. After was when it carried weight.

So where was he?

And why did she have this awful, sick feeling in the pit of her stomach, this uneasy sensation that something was very, very wrong?

As Natalie shifted to swing her legs out of bed, she saw it. Just beneath his pillow—*his* pillow—there was a bit of paper peeking out.

Natalie froze.

She wanted to leave it there. To ignore it. Because the moment she acknowledged it was the moment she had to read it. And the moment she read it, she knew that the euphoric state she'd allowed herself to slip into would burst apart like a soap bubble that had floated on the breeze a second too long, done in by the very thing that had made it float.

But she was Natalie Rothchild. Natalie, the sensible one. The one who faced her problems and life in general head on and fearlessly. Natalie, the rebel who refused to allow her family's vast fortune to keep her from living a life of purpose.

Matt told her that was one of the things he loved about her.

He *loved* her.

Didn't he?

Pressing her lips together, steeling herself, Natalie pulled the note out from beneath the pillow. She held it in her trembling hands and forced herself to read it.

Her eyes clouded with tears, nearly blinding her before she finished.

Balling up the paper, she threw it across the room and then buried her face against her raised knees. Her heart broken, Natalie did what she rarely did. She surrendered to despair.

Quiet sobs filled the silence within the room.

She was really alone.

Chapter 1

Excitement vibrated through Candace Rothchild's veins. She could literally *feel* her adrenaline accelerating. Creating a rush. It was always this way when she stepped out in front of the cameras. Being the center of attention— even *anticipating* being the center of attention created a high that few drugs, legal or otherwise, could equal. Ever since she could remember, Candace thrived on the lime- light, ate it up as if it was a source of energy for her.

Unlike her twin sister, Natalie, whom she considered a dull, placid being with little imagination or flair, Candace positively bloomed when attention was thrown her way. The bigger, the better had always been her motto.

To this end, she always made sure that she was picture perfect. She wore the latest fashions, had the kind of figure women would kill for and men remem- bered long after she had passed out of their lives. If, at times, that necessitated starving herself and spending outrageous amounts of money, well, so be it. It was all worth it. She wasn't cut out for the tranquil, humdrum life. Which meant the role of doting mother, to sons she hardly knew and had less time for, wasn't for her. The only plus from that end was that the tabloids were forever attempting to guess who had fathered them and if, indeed, it had been the same man in both cases.

Beyond that, the children—Mick and David, named after her favorite singers—held no interest for her. Far more important was that there was always another premiere, another function, another occasion to be photographed and fawned over. At times, she would imagine average, desperate women hungrily devouring the tidbits of her life, fantasizing about the men she'd bedded, all in an effort to leave, however briefly, their own drab lives behind.

She was doing a public service living this way, Candace told herself, a smirk twisting her ripe, collagen-full lips. She gave those poor, hopeless women something to dream about.

Why, she was positively noble, if you gave it any thought, Candace silently congratulated herself as she gracefully slid out of the backseat of the limousine and onto the red carpet that was unfurled before The Janus. This opulent casino, where tonight's charity gala was being held, was Luke Montgomery's most extravagant enterprise to date. Never mind that Luke and her father were rivals the way only the nouveau riche could be in Las Vegas, where the stakes that ran highest were not always found on a blackjack table.

The gala Luke was hosting centered around an international jewelry convention. On display was a breath-taking collection of gems that had been donated by various members of the rich and famous, all in the name of charity. The price of admission was high but only in terms of what the average person could afford.

The sum meant nothing to Candace. Money had never been a problem for her. Sustaining her high had been—because she needed to stay in the spotlight in order to survive. Without it, the insecurities that lingered in the background began to encroach, darkening her world and threatening to sink her into a nether region fraught with madness.

So she did what she could to ensure that she would never descend to those levels. She surrounded herself with glamorous people and basked in the glow of the limelight the way no one else could.

Charity or not, Candace had no gems she was willing to part with. She never met an expensive bauble she didn't immediately love. And tonight, she was sporting the best of the best, a legendary diamond that, according to a rumor she'd heard, had been in her family for several decades. The Tears of the Quetzal. Only gems of quality had names, she thought with a smug grin.

Her father, Harold Rothchild, thought the ring was safely under lock and key. But then, he had no idea how determined she could be. Or how clever. Like everyone else, he had underestimated her. His problem, she thought carelessly.

Besides, what good was jewelry if you couldn't wear it? Couldn't flaunt it and make others look at it enviously? None, that's what. Jewelry had to be seen to be appreciated.

And its owner envied.

Candace looked down now at the ring on her hand. The incredible multifaceted diamond captured all the light in the immediate vicinity and flashed it back onto her in bursts of green and purple. It was as if she had a star on her ring finger. Rumor had it that there was a curse attached to it.

All nonsense, she was certain. The so-called curse was started by her father, or maybe Grandpa Joe before him to keep people from making off with the gem. But she wasn't ignorant like the rest of her pathetic family.

She had no concerns about a curse, only about the attention wearing the priceless gem could garner her. She stood for a moment as the limousine pulled away, letting those in the immediate vicinity drink in the sight of her. She gave the appearance of being taller than she was, helped, in part, by stiletto heels. The long, clinging scarlet gown she wore would have been eye-catching under any circumstances. On her it was doubly so, and she knew it. Cascading platinum hair completed the picture. She was a knockout.

She was alone tonight. Deliberately so. She wanted to be unencumbered as she scanned the sea of men this gala had lured. She wanted to be free to scan them and to bring the one that pleased her most back to her condo. Her sons had been packed off with the nanny for an overnight visit with the nanny's sister and nephews—which left the terrain open for her. There would be no disapproving nanny, no annoying children popping up at inopportune times to ask even more annoying questions.

She was in the mood for something new tonight. Something different. Exotic, perhaps.

Exotic, yes.

A smile slipped over her lips as she slowly made her way along the carpet, her pace timed to the flashes that were going off, marking her passage. Photographers called out her name and vied for better positions in order to snare the "perfect" photograph.

In a pinch, Candace mused, she might not mind reverting back to the tried and true. Like Luke Montgomery. In his time, he'd been very hot in bed. Hot enough to leave an impression on her in his wake, even now. Not an easy feat considering the number of lovers she'd had over the years. Her collection had begun at the precocious age of fourteen when she'd surrendered her virginity, already rather compromised, to the family chauffeur. Paolo, as she recalled, had been poor, but beautiful.

And very, very skilled in the ways of lovemaking.

She wondered where Paolo was these days. Her father had gotten rid of the driver the moment he'd found out about the affair. Harold Rothchild had indignantly threatened the man with prison, but even she'd known that the threat was empty. Ever conscious of their reputation, her father wanted nothing more than to avoid any sort of public scandal that reflected poorly on the family.

She'd given him quite a run for his money, she thought, turning her face up so that the lighting caught her just so.

"Poor Dad, you should have raised prize-winning roses, not daughters," she mused under her breath.

Recognizing them, she paused to pose for several national magazine photographers. One hand on her hip, the other—the one with the ring—delicately placed just beneath her collarbone and above the deeply plunging neckline that left only the tiniest speck to the imagination. Of the two of them, she wondered which was more of a disappointment to her father, she with her penchant of attracting every photographer within a fifty-mile radius, or Natalie, who worked as a police detective, for God sakes. How mundane and common can you get?

"This way, Candace. Look this way!" a deep male voice called out urgently.

The voice, she noted, sounded vaguely familiar to her, although she doubted she could place it as she turned in the direction it had come from.

And then she smiled more brilliantly. She was right. She *had* recognized the voice. Recognized the man as well, although she couldn't remember his name.

Something beginning with a *P,* she thought, although she couldn't be sure. Or maybe it began with a *B*. But then, it didn't matter if she remembered them, only that they remembered her, and by the look on this one's face, he most certainly did remember her.

They'd slept together, hadn't they? she thought. He looked like her type. Tall, muscular, with an olive complexion, thick black hair and high cheekbones that gave him almost an aristocratic look. She might have mistaken him for one of the invited guests—if not for the camera he was clutching.

But he was exotic looking and she really was in the mood for someone exotic.

"What have you got for us, Candace?" he called out, elbowing his way forward ahead of the gaggle of photographers. Grumbling and curses marked his forward progress.

"A lot of sugar," she answered in a breathless voice that made her sound as if she were channeling the spirit of the late Marilyn Monroe at her zenith. "And, of course, this."

"This" was the ring that she now held up like a courtesan in the court of King Henry VIII waiting to have her hand kissed. A satisfied smirk graced her lips again. A flurry of cameras went off, capturing the image and the moment.

But her attention was only focused on the photographer with the aura of danger about him. Winking, she bent forward, giving him, she knew, ample view of her endowment.

"Didn't we...?" Candace deliberately let her voice trail off even as her eyes held him prisoner in their blue gaze.

His smile, she caught herself thinking, was incredibly sexy as he answered in a low voice, "Yes, we did. I'm flattered that you remembered."

It was the perfect thing to say to her and he knew it, even as he maintained his innocent expression.

Candace did her best to recall the details of their coupling—and failed. "I'm afraid your name..." She shrugged playfully, a laugh escaping her carefully made up lips. "I was never good with names."

"Patrick," he supplied politely, snapping another photograph. She preened. "My name's Patrick Moore."

"I *knew* it was something that started with the letter *P*," she declared triumphantly.

It took effort for the photographer to keep his true feelings from showing on his face. It took even more effort to keep from telling this two-bit slut what he thought of her and her whole degenerate family. But then, that would have been counterproductive to his plan. He hoped that by supplying her with the name he was going by these days, it would keep her from thinking too much. From remembering.

But then, he comforted himself, her brain usually oscillated between being fried or being pickled. Neither state was conducive to remembering pertinent details, like the ones that would blow his cover.

"Is the ring yours now?" someone else, obviously at least mildly familiar with the ring's chain of ownership, called out to Candace.

She didn't bother trying to hide the condescending glance she sent toward the photographer. Her laughter echoed with victory.

"It's always been mine," she announced.

Out of the corner of her eye she caught a glimpse of Luke just within the entrance. Six foot two, lean and muscular, with dark hair she remembered running her fingers through, he looked incredible. A touch of nostalgia surfaced. He always did look good in a tux.

Looked damn good out of one, too, she thought with a lascivious smile.

"If you gentlemen'll excuse me," she murmured to the reporters. And then, because she hated the prospect of facing the night in an empty bed, she glanced back at the exotic reporter. It never hurt to have an ace in the hole. "Maybe we can get together later. I'll fill you in on what I've been doing lately. For your tabloid," she added with a wink as she patted his face, her ring sparkling and throwing off beams of light with every movement.

"I'd like that," he told her.

She expected nothing less. "Yes, I'm sure you would. I'm staying at—"

"I know where you're staying," Patrick Moore cut her short.

She smiled, inclining her head. "Clever boy," she murmured.

With that, she sashayed off to the casino, every step a calculated movement guaranteed to make men's mouths water.

Once inside, Candace began to move just a tad faster. If she'd retained her present pace, the object of her pursuit, Luke Montgomery, would have put too much distance between them. She very much wanted to hook up with the gala host. Men of power were like an aphrodisiac for her, and Luke Montgomery, despite his humble beginnings, was now regarded as one of Vegas's movers and shakers. Nothing she liked more than being on the winning team.

She had, she liked to think, a lot to bring to the table.

"Luke," she called out to him. When he didn't appear to hear her, Candace raised her voice, temporarily abandoning Marilyn Monroe's sexy, throaty whisper for pragmatic reasons. There was still no response.

The third time she called out his name, Luke stopped walking. He could feel his shoulders tensing. He'd heard her the first time and had hoped that she would just give up.

He should have known better.

Damn that shrew anyway. He wanted the focus of this gala to be on him, his newest casino and the charity he was sponsoring, in that order. Nowhere in that hierarchy did he want to include a vapid, superficial bleach-blonde.

But if he didn't acknowledge her, he knew she was going to cause a scene, and that was the last thing he wanted tonight.

So Luke turned around, a perfunctory smile of civility on his lips worn for the benefit of anyone who might be passing by.

"Hello, Candace," he said as soon as he crossed back to her. Towering over the woman, he all but quietly growled, "I don't seem to remember sending you an invitation."

A careless laugh met his statement. "I'm sure it was just an oversight." Candace possessively threaded her arms through his. Being so close to Luke vividly reminded her of the last time they'd been together. Though she'd never said anything, she'd considered settling down with him. At least for a while. A lady-killer who lived up to his reputation, he was a magnificent lover who always left her wanting more.

Because she sensed that this gala meant a lot to him, she tried to get on his good side by saying, "This certainly has the looks of being quite a successful event."

He certainly hoped so. Luke had undertaken hosting this event and pulling together all the beautiful people from the four corners of the world not just to benefit the charity he was sponsoring but also because hosting such an event, where all the rich and famous showed up in droves, would garner him an enormous amount of goodwill. Good publicity was crucial since he was on the verge of building yet another casino and hotel—this one on the exact spot where the tenement building he'd lived in as a child had stood.

The Phoenix, as the new establishment would be

called, was very near and dear to him, and he wanted nothing to hamper its success. Someone like Candace Rothchild and the kind of attention she attracted could do a lot of harm to all his good intentions.

He wanted her out of here, and he had no time to be polite about it. Moving over to a more private corner of the casino, he asked in a controlled, low voice, "What is it you want, Candace?"

Her eyes raked over his body, blatantly undressing him as she looked up into his eyes. "Why, darling, that should be very evident to someone as smart as you." Tightening her hold on his arm, Candace raised her face up to his. Her mouth was barely inches away from his lips. "You."

Gone were the days when he would have been flattered. He knew her for what she was. A woman with no soul on her way out, living in a town that didn't care. She was swiftly becoming a punch line to a good many insulting jokes.

"Not now, Candace."

A pout appeared on her moist lips. "Then when?" she wanted to know.

What had he ever seen in her? he couldn't help wondering. Granted, there'd been a time when he would have gladly taken her up on her offer, but he'd been younger then and far more impressionable. He'd like to think he was too smart now to be tempted to lie down with a black widow.

He shook his arm free and then grasped hers. He began directing her toward the front entrance. "Some other time, Candace," he said forcefully.

Instantly, her face clouded over. "I don't like being

rejected, Luke. Your little party won't go so well if I make a scene. That's what they'll remember, *me,*" she emphasized, "not you or this little jewelry store display of yours."

It was a threat with teeth, and they both knew it.

He didn't react well to threats. "I think you'll be happier elsewhere, Candace," Luke told her coldly. He snapped his fingers over her head at someone across the floor.

She didn't bother looking to see who Luke was summoning. She wasn't interested.

"And I think I'll be happier here," she insisted. Accustomed to getting her way, it infuriated her to be contradicted.

The next moment, they were joined by a third party. Matt Schaffer, the head of security for Montgomery Enterprises, was at her elbow. But rather than look at her, his attention was completely focused on his employer. Matt waited silently for instructions.

Candace always perked up when in the company of a good-looking man, and this time was no exception as recognition entered her eyes.

"Why, hello handsome," she purred.

Candace had already had too much to drink, Matt realized. He could smell it on her. But he was careful not to allow his disdain to register on his face. Instead, he raised his eyes to Luke's face.

"Mr. Montgomery?"

"Schaffer, please escort Ms. Rothchild out of the casino," Luke requested, his voice flat and devoid of emotion. "She was just leaving."

Candace became incensed. "No, I wasn't," she insisted heatedly. She gave every impression that she was about to dig in her heels, and if Matt intended to remove her, it was going to have to be by force.

But rather than take hold of her arm and drag her from the premises, cursing and screaming, Matt leaned over and whispered into her ear. "There are a bunch of photographers outside asking about you," he told the Rothchild heiress smoothly. "You wouldn't want to disappoint your public, would you?"

Her blue eyes flashed, reminding him of another pair of blue eyes. Matt banked down the memory and the feelings it threatened to usher in with it. He'd made his choice, and he had to live with it...*had* been living with it these last eight years.

"*I* don't want to be disappointed," Candace told him haughtily.

There was another, more logical approach to this. "You'll save face if you make it look as if leaving is your idea. Ms. Rothchild," Matt told her quietly. "But make no mistake, one way or another, you *are* leaving the casino."

Candace exhaled angrily, then, right before his eyes, she managed to get herself under control. There was a squadron of cameras waiting to capture her beautiful likeness, she thought, and she knew that when she frowned, she looked closer to her own age. Thirty was a horrible number.

As she moved toward the door, Candace thought she could see that reporter—the sexy one—looking in her direction. Patrick Moore.

Something told her that the evening was not going to be a total waste after all.

She flashed a radiant smile. "I'll have your head," she

promised Matt through lips that looked as if they were barely moving.

They were almost at the entrance, but Matt knew better than to release her. If he did, she might just double back, and he needed her on the other side of the door.

"From what I hear," he told her conversationally, "that's not the part that interests you when it comes to men."

They made brief eye contact. Just like that, her fury was gone. The smile on Candace's lips was genuine. "I know you, but I can't seem to remember your name."

He saw no point in refusing to answer. From what he knew, she and Natalie hadn't spoken in a long, long time. She wouldn't tell Natalie about this. "Matt Schaffer."

Candace nodded her head, as if absorbing the name. "Right. Of course you are."

Matt pushed the door open for her. He watched the woman saunter away and swiftly become engulfed by the crowd hanging around the casino entrance. She was in her element.

As he walked back into the casino, Matt could only shake his head. The woman he'd just escorted out was light years away from Natalie. Hard to believe they were actually sisters, much less twins.

The next moment, he forced himself to think of something else. Thinking about Natalie would do him no good. That part of his life was over.

By choice.

Chapter 2

She had to be out of her mind, Anna Worth Rothchild thought.

It was past eleven o'clock, and by all rights, she should have been in bed. The all-night parties that Vegas was so famous for no longer interested her. They never really had, but she'd pretended they did for his sake. Now, instead of curling up in her queen-sized bed, sleeping peacefully, here she was pulling up into her old driveway. Summoned by the distraught note in her ex-husband's voice when he'd called her less than an hour ago.

She was an idiot for doing this.

What she should have said to him, Anna silently lectured herself as she got out of her ice-blue sports car, was "Tell it to your little bimbo, Rebecca Lynn. Whatever's wrong in your life isn't my problem anymore."

But that was just it—it *was* still her problem. Her

problem because she chose it to be. And that, sadly, was because reasonable, independent woman that she was, she nevertheless still loved the man. Loved him despite the fact that he had, as the old jazz songs went, "done her wrong."

There was a term for women like her, Anna mused, and if she had half a brain, she'd turn around, get back into her car and drive back home. There was no reason for her to be here.

Yes, between the two of them, they had four daughters in common. Anna's natural child, Silver, was her ex-husband's daughter whom Harold later adopted. Silver grew up in the vicinity of three stepsisters from Harold's first marriage—twins Natalie and Candace and their younger sister Jenna. Raising these girls together would forever bind Anna and Harold to one another. But he had made it perfectly clear he wanted to spend the rest of his life with that gold-digging slut who was only four years older than his twin daughters. He deserved everything that happened to him for being such a fool. For throwing away their marriage after all the years she'd stood by his side, taking care of every detail, leaving him free to handle his businesses and his hotels.

So why was she here? Why did she even *care* if Harold was distraught?

Because she did, Anna thought with a sigh, wrapping her ermine stole tighter around her shoulders against the April evening chill. It was as simple as that. She just did.

About to ring the doorbell, she was caught off guard when the door suddenly swung open and Clive, Harold's butler for the past twenty-five years, firmly ushered out a tall, dark-haired man with an olive complexion. The well-built, exotic-looking man was far from happy to be leaving the premises. Although he was wearing formal attire, it appeared somewhat rumpled.

The intruder nearly knocked her down as he was being hustled out of the mansion. The unexpected close contact allowed Anna to catch the faintest whiff of a sweet scent. It was vaguely familiar and nudged something distant in her consciousness, but she couldn't place it.

The next moment, the memory was gone. The thought that the scent was something a woman might wear whispered through her mind as she regained her balance. The latter was accomplished largely due to Clive's swift action. Seeing her predicament, he quickly caught the former mistress of the mansion by the arm and kept her from falling.

"Sorry, ma'am, didn't mean to be forward," he apologized, withdrawing his hands the moment she regained her footing.

Anna smiled. After all these years with the family, Clive was still incredibly formal. She sincerely doubted that they made people, much less butlers, like him anymore.

"Apology more than accepted, Clive. If you hadn't caught me, that oaf would have mowed me down." She glanced over her shoulder and saw the stranger was retreating through the gate. She decided the man had to belong to the car that was parked down the street. "What was that all about?"

"I'm sure I don't know, ma'am. He's one of those ruthless reporters, I believe." Anna was certain that Clive knew far more than he was saying. Nothing happened in this house or to this family that the gray-haired man was not aware of. "So nice to see you again, ma'am," he said warmly, deftly changing the topic. "Mr. Harold is expecting you. He's in the den."

The butler dutifully escorted her to the room. Along the way she noted some changes. There were expensive, somewhat showy, paintings gracing the walls. Rebecca Lynn's handiwork, no doubt, she mused. If there was a spare dime lying around, the woman would find something to spend it on.

Opening the den's double doors for her, Clive unobtrusively backed away and withdrew, moving as silently as a shadow.

Harold, his back to her, was alone in the room. When he turned around, she was struck by how drawn he looked. His hand was wrapped tightly around a chunky scotch glass. The glass was almost empty.

Her first thought was that something had happened with the eye candy he referred to as his third wife. Had she been a lesser woman, she might have secretly gloated at the thought. But Anna was made of better stuff than that, and she found her heart aching for him, aching despite the fact that he had been less than kind during the final days of their marriage.

"All right, Harold, I'm here," she declared, crossing to him. Removing her wrap, she carefully draped it over the back of the cream-colored leather sofa. "What's the big emergency that couldn't wait until morning?"

On his best day, Harold Rothchild was never one of those men who exuded power. What power he had he inherited from a father who had been almighty, leaving no room for a son to emerge and become his own man, even if he was handsome enough to turn a few heads. All his life, Harold had searched for a way to do that, to become his own man. Years after Joseph Rothchild's death, Harold was still searching.

Draining his glass, he placed it on the desk and cleared his throat before finally giving her an answer. He felt a tightness in his chest. "It's gone."

He wasn't making any sense, and there was panic evident in his blue eyes. Anna put her hand on her ex-husband's, as if to silently reassure him that she was there for him. "What's gone, Harold?"

"The ring." His voice seemed to crackle with the stress he was experiencing. "My father's ring. The Tears of the Quetzal. Candace kept asking me questions about it. When she asked to see it, I said no. I thought she'd get angry, but she just said, 'All right.' After she left, I had this feeling that something was wrong," he confessed, almost talking to himself. "So I went to the safe to look at it—and it was gone," he wailed. "And now something bad is going to happen. I can feel it. Something awful."

Anna didn't follow him, but then, Harold had always been secretive when it came to the ring and its origins. All she had ever gotten out of him was that, in the right hands, it brought true love to its owner within sixty seconds. In the wrong hands, dire things came to pass. Personally, she'd always thought it was all just empty talk, something to glorify the ring, nothing more. She'd only seen it once herself, and it was far too gaudy for her taste.

"Worse than the ring disappearing?" she asked.

Harold seemed to go pale right in front of her eyes. A line of sweat formed on his forehead. He sounded almost breathless when he said, "Much worse."

Natalie Rothchild felt sick to her stomach. It took all she had to keep the light breakfast down that she'd consumed this morning.

After working her way up within the Las Vegas Police Department to the rank of detective in a relatively short amount of time, there weren't many things that still got to her. She'd learned to harden herself, to separate herself from her work. She kept a firm, if imaginary, line drawn in the sand for herself. Her professional life was not allowed to cross over into her personal life—what little there was of it.

Natalie was well aware that if she began to take her work home with her, she would burn out within six months—the way Sid Northrop, one of the homicide detectives on the force when she'd first joined it, had.

But this was different. This *was* personal. And she hadn't been summoned to the scene because it was personal. She'd come because she'd overheard the dispatch put the call out on the police scanner. According to the information, a hysterical nanny had come home with her two charges only to find the children's mother dead on the living room floor. Natalie was about to ignore it because two other detectives were being called in to handle the homicide and God knew she had enough on her plate already without being Johnny-on-the-spot for yet another murder.

But the address that the dispatch rattled off stopped her cold. The address belonged to Candace.

A wave of fear mingled with disbelief washed over her. Her hands felt icy as she held onto the steering wheel. Even though she and her sister lived in two different worlds and didn't interact, she still felt an obligation to keep tabs on Candace. Her twin sister had cotton candy for brains, not to mention that Candace's self-esteem was like a giant champagne bucket with a hole in the bottom. She seemed in desperate need of adulation and found it living her life on the wild side.

If anyone needed a keeper, it was Candace. And even though they no longer had anything in common but blood, Natalie secretly had appointed herself her sister's protector, keeping Candace out of harm's way whenever she possibly could.

Damn, but she'd really dropped the ball this time, Natalie upbraided herself grimly.

In Candace's condo now, she fought back anguished tears as she looked down at her sister's battered face and body. The room looked like a battlefield, and Candace was lying on the floor next to the marble coffee table, her limbs spread out in a grotesque, awkward fashion like a cartoon character that hadn't been drawn correctly. The scarlet dress that Candace had undoubtedly paid a fortune for accented the pool of blood that encircled her head lying on the ivory rug.

"You shouldn't be here," a gruff voice behind her admonished.

She blinked twice, banishing her tears before she glanced over her shoulder at Adam Parker, one of the two detectives who had been called in.

"Yeah, well, neither should she," Natalie bit off angrily.

Reaching out, she adjusted the right side of the front of Candace's dress to cover her exposed breast.

"Hey, you know better than to touch anything," Miles Davidson, the other detective, pointed out, crossing over to her.

Yes, she knew better. But this was her sister, and at least in death, Candace needed a little respect.

"I just wanted to cover her," Natalie answered quietly, rising to her feet. It didn't matter that, at one time or another, half of Vegas had probably seen Candace naked; she didn't want this being the final impression those processing the scene came away with. Taking a cleansing breath, Natalie looked over toward Parker, the older and far more heavyset of the two detectives. "What have you got?"

His frustrated expression answered before he did. "You got here fifteen minutes after we did. Nothing so far," he replied somberly. "The ME can answer a few basic questions for us once he gets her on the table." Natalie continued to look at him expectantly. The ME had been on the scene when she arrived. Parker exhaled sharply. "Right now, it looks like time of death was around eight, maybe nine o'clock last night. We looked around and robbery doesn't seem to have been a motive. Nothing's been taken." He pointed toward Candace's throat. "She's still wearing a diamond necklace." A weary sigh escaped his lips. "Judging by her bruises and the state of this room, I'd say this was personal."

Squatting down again, Natalie looked at her twin's right hand. Last night, while heating up a frozen dinner, she'd kept the TV on for background noise. A program devoted to fawning over celebrities had been on, and they had gushed over live film clips from the gala in progress at The Janus.

She hadn't been surprised to see Candace on camera. Candace had a penchant for showing up anywhere that a camera was rolling. What had surprised her was that her twin was flashing the Tears of the Quetzal, holding it up for the camera to capture. Natalie knew for a fact that her father kept the ring under lock and key, refusing even to allow any of them to see it, much less flaunt it in public.

How had Candace managed to get it away from their father?

And who had taken it off Candace's finger?

"The ring's gone," she told Parker quietly.

"Ring? What ring?" Davidson blinked, suddenly looking more alert.

Parker didn't need to ask. Natalie knew he was already aware of what she was referring to. "You mean that big golf ball-sized rock that your dad's got hidden away in some faraway safe?" When his partner looked at him in surprise, Parker shrugged the wide shoulders beneath his worn all-weather coat. "What? I read *People* magazine. Sue me."

"That's the one," Natalie replied with a sigh, standing up again. Her grandfather, Joseph, had owned the diamond mine from which the multifaceted, near priceless gem had emerged, or so she had heard from her stepmother. Her father's fortune was partially built on it.

Did he kill you for it, Candace? Did whoever did this to you try to take the ring only to have you fight him off? You should have let him have it. It was a stupid rock…it wasn't worth your life.

A thought suddenly hit her, and she looked up at the two detectives. "Anyone notify my father yet?"

Parker and Davidson exchanged looks. She had her answer. Notification of a loved one's death was never high on anyone's to-do list.

"Not yet," Parker answered grimly.

Natalie nodded, already resigned to her part in this. "I'll do it. Let me know what the ME comes up with as soon as there's a report."

Parker frowned, but his tone was kind as he tried to make her understand his position. "Natalie, we can't have you—"

She stopped him before he could finish voicing his protest. "Unofficially," she emphasized. "Notify me unofficially." There was no room for argument in her voice. She looked around. "Where are the kids?"

"Kids?" Davis echoed.

"Kids," she repeated. "Candace's kids. Mick and David. My sister has—had—two children. Dispatch said the nanny found her and called this in. Where are they?"

"Take it easy. She took them back to her sister's house. Don't worry, Sanchez went with her," Parker said, mentioning another detective. "Um, correct me if I'm wrong, but from what I heard, your sister really didn't keep close tabs on her kids."

"No, she didn't." She needed to get in touch with the nanny, Natalie thought as she left.

She had the woman's name and number programmed into her cell phone. She'd already checked out Amelia Pintero's background to satisfy herself that her young nephews were in good hands—and not because Candace had asked her to. Candace, as she recalled, was just glad to have someone else take care of them for her. She would have used Gypsies if they'd crossed her path before Amelia had.

Natalie knew that it was a given that she wouldn't be allowed to investigate her sister's murder, but there was no law that said she couldn't look into it on her own when she was off duty. And even if there was, there was no way she was about to abide by the restriction. She and Candace hadn't gotten along in a long time, but blood was blood and after all was said and done, Candace was still her sister. More, she'd been her twin. A part of her was dead.

She deserved some answers—and the killer deserved to be put away for the rest of his life. It was as simple as that. And she planned to kick off her investigation by going to The Janus, the casino where Candace was last seen. She was going to have to find a way to get a look at the security tapes, to see if someone had followed her sister when she left the casino—or if, and this scenario was far more likely, Candace had elected to leave the casino with someone new.

In her heart, Natalie had always known that men would be her sister's downfall.

And that makes you different how? a mocking tone in her head queried. For her, it hadn't taken a squadron of men; all it had taken was one. One man who had sworn his love for her, given her an engagement ring and then pulled a disappearing act.

It had made her back away from the entire species.

Damn, she hadn't thought about Matt in, what? A couple of months or so.

Now was not the time for a stroll down memory lane, Natalie chided herself as she pulled up in her father's winding driveway.

Natalie took a deep breath, bracing herself for the ordeal ahead. It didn't really help.

With effort, she got out of her car.

The walk from the driveway to the front door felt exceptionally drawn out and almost painful, a little like a prisoner walking the last mile before his execution, she mused.

Clive answered the door. He smiled at her, looking both formal and kind at the same time. It was a feat she never quite understood how he accomplished. A pleased light entered his hazel eyes. "Miss Natalie, what a pleasant surprise."

She knew he meant it. For a second, she allowed herself to absorb his words, and then she set her mouth solemnly. "Not so pleasant I'm afraid, Clive. Is my father home?"

To his credit, Clive displayed no curiosity, asked no questions. "Yes he is, Miss, but I fear that he doesn't seem to be himself today."

Natalie looked at the butler in surprise. Had her father heard about Candace? But how? The police were keeping everything under wraps for now. Their main logic behind this was to stave off the media vultures for as long as possible. They could feed on this kind of fodder for six, nine months at a time. And they would. But right now, they weren't supposed to know.

Had there been a leak?

"Why?" she pressed. "What's wrong, Clive?"

She knew that the man was very closemouthed, but

she also knew that while she'd lived in this cold mausoleum of a house, she had been his favorite. So she looked up at the tall man and waited for a response.

It came. "It's the Tears of the Quetzal, Miss. I'm afraid that someone seems to have made off with it."

An image of Candace, flaunting the ring in front of the cameraman, flashed through her mind. It was immediately followed by the sight of her lifeless body lying on the rug, her hand denuded of the legendary ring.

"You can say that again," she murmured under her breath. "Where is he?"

"He's on the terrace, Miss. He's been there for most of the night. I tried to get him to come in, but…" His voice trailed off.

"You're a good man, Clive. But some people won't allow themselves to be helped." She was talking about Candace—not her father—but for now, it was applicable to him as well.

Turning, Natalie made her way to the back of the house, no small feat. As far as houses went, she'd always felt that this one could have provided shelter to a small third world country. Neither she nor her stepmother, Anna, had cared for its enormity, but Candace had loved it and her father's current wife, Rebecca Lynn, the world's only living brain donor, had actually been lobbying for something even bigger and more ostentatious.

Maybe the Taj Mahal was up for sale, Natalie thought sarcastically. She could remember thinking when they first moved to this house that she needed to drop bread crumbs to mark her way or be forever doomed to wandering the halls, looking for the way out.

She'd found the way out years ago.

Finally reaching the back of the building, she walked out onto the terrace. She was immediately struck by her father's profile as he sat at the table. He was still a handsome man, Natalie caught herself thinking. But right now, he looked gaunt and incredibly weary, as if he had the weight of the world on his shoulders.

That was Rebecca Lynn's fault, no doubt. He was trying to keep up with a woman half his age who was determined to "do it all." Either that, or become a young widow. God knew she wouldn't put it past Rebecca Lynn.

She didn't say anything until she was almost at his elbow. "Hi, Dad."

She'd startled him. He sucked in his breath, his body tense and rigid. "Natalie, what are you doing here?"

There was no point in beating around the bush. It only prolonged the inevitable, and that wasn't her style. "I have some terrible news, Dad." Natalie sat down at the table and placed her hand over his. Her father wasn't the touchy-feely type, but this time, she thought some contact might actually help. "Candace is dead."

He visibly paled but didn't look nearly as surprised as she thought he would. She supposed that, given Candace's lifestyle, all of them had been expecting this day now for a long time. "When?"

"Last night."

He slowly nodded his head, as if that helped him take in the information. "Where?"

"They found her body at her condo. The nanny came home with the kids after a sleepover and discovered her. She called the police." She enunciated the words slowly, refusing to allow her voice to break, her emotions to leak through. Her feelings were private, even from her father. "Candace was murdered."

It took Harold a moment to process the information she'd given him, and then he looked up at her, his expression devoid of emotion. "Did she have the ring on her?"

"Ring?" Natalie repeated, stunned. She remembered what Clive had said about her father's distress because the ring was missing. Candace was dead. Didn't that trump a missing ring? Didn't he care? "Is that what you're concerned about?" she cried, struggling to keep her temper under control. "The damn ring?"

He grew more upset in the face of her reaction. "Natalie, please understand, of course I'm devastated about Candace, but that ring…that ring can mean the difference between our family's financial collapse and success."

How could he even think about money at a time like this? "What are you talking about?"

Harold nervously ran his tongue along his dry lips. "I made some shaky investments," he confessed. "I'm spread rather thin right now, and I had to borrow some money from—" He paused for a moment before finally blurting out a name. "The Schaffer family."

He'd been desperate at the time; there was no other explanation for his doing what he'd done. He didn't have his father's flair for making money, so he'd turned to a family known to have underworld connections. Men who broke legs as easily as matchsticks and with less thought. He wouldn't put it past Matt Schaffer to try to ruin him.

His eyes grew bright. "Matt Schaffer's the one who has the ring. I'd bet my life on it," he concluded heatedly.

She hadn't thought she'd ever hear that name again.

"Matt Schaffer's in California," she heard herself saying hoarsely.

And then her father blew her world apart by saying, "No, he's not. He's right here in Vegas. Working for Luke Montgomery. Or at least that's the story he gives out."

Matt Schaffer.

Here. In Vegas.

Natalie suddenly felt as if the ground beneath her feet had turned to quicksand.

Chapter 3

Harold continued to talk, but Natalie could no longer make out the words.

Her father's voice became a buzzing sound in the background as she grappled with the information he'd just carelessly flung out at her. Coming on the heels of Candace's murder, learning that Matt Schaffer was now living back in Vegas was almost too much for her to process. Or bear.

But she had to, Natalie told herself fiercely. What choice did she have? There was no one around to run interference for her, no one to try to smooth out the choppy waters so she could navigate them without going under and drowning.

All that was on her shoulders. But then, she'd more or less been on her own for the last eight years.

Natalie raised her chin proudly. Okay, she'd deal

with Matt being here in Vegas. Deal with having to see him.

But despite the way things had ended between them, she knew Matt Schaffer would never kill anyone. If he had the ring in his possession, then he'd gotten a hold of it while Candace was still alive. She'd make book on it.

You also thought he'd never leave you, remember? Called that one wrong, didn't you? her annoying little voice taunted.

Still, just because the man didn't have the guts to commit and lacked the backbone to tell her so face-to-face didn't mean he would kill someone over a ring no matter how valuable it was. He wasn't a killer or a thief, if she discounted his stealing her heart.

"Matt wouldn't kill Candace," she told her father firmly.

Her father looked like a cornered man desperately fighting to survive. He vacillated, not sure of anything anymore.

"Maybe not, but someone in his family would." Everyone knew that the Schaffers had underworld ties, connections to people who did things that could not bear scrutiny. He grasped her hand as if that would make her understand better. "I *owe* them, Natalie. I owe them." Harold struggled to keep his voice from cracking. "The Schaffers know people. And those people," he insisted, "have killed for pocket change."

She glared at him. "Then *why* would you have knowingly gotten mixed up with them?" she demanded.

It made no sense to her. There were lending institutions. Yes, money was hard to come by, but Harold Rothchild was a reputable businessman with a great deal of collateral. Going to a loan shark, if that was indeed what he'd done, was like agreeing to play Russian roulette with not one but half the chambers loaded with bullets.

"Because…" He began to explain, then stopped abruptly. "Oh, it doesn't matter why. I did, and now Candace is dead and the ring's gone."

Her father seemed to have forgotten one very important element in this horrible tale. So typical of him, she thought.

"Your nephews are fine, thanks for asking," she told him sarcastically. She'd checked on the boys on her way over here. She'd stopped by the nanny's sister's home and asked Amelia to tell her in her own words what she'd seen. She had to wait until the young woman stopped throwing up. The details were sketchy, the nanny's reaction honest. She'd asked the young woman to watch the boys until she got back to her.

"The boys." Harold stared at her for a moment, a lost look in his eyes. And then he seemed to come to. "Where are they?"

"I left them with their nanny." She rattled off the address. It was far off the beaten path of both the casinos and the better residential areas, but it was still a decent-enough neighborhood, thanks to a renovation effort on the part of the city.

"I'll send a car for them," Harold said, thinking out loud.

"Good idea."

She didn't mean that to sound as caustic as it did. But she was on edge. The toughest part of her day was still ahead of her. She was going to have to go and interface with the one man she didn't want to ever see again.

Some days it just didn't pay to get up out of bed, Natalie thought wearily.

About to say goodbye, something in her father's expression stopped her. She knew it would drive her crazy for the rest of the day if she didn't ask. "Is there something else?" she wanted to know. "You look like you want to tell me something."

"No." Denial was always his first choice, but then Harold thought better of it just as his daughter began to leave. "There was a note."

Natalie turned around. What was he talking about? And why hadn't he said anything when she'd first come in? "A note?"

He nodded his head. "I didn't understand what it meant until you told me that Candace was dead." He sounded breathless as he said, "We're all in danger. The curse is real."

Natalie looked at her father as if he'd lost his mind. It took considerable effort to remain patient. "You're talking in riddles, Dad. Start at the beginning. *What* note?"

Rather than continue trying to explain, Harold took a folded piece of paper out of the pocket of his robe and handed it to her. She noticed that his hand shook a little.

"This was in the mailbox this morning. Clive found it when he went to put in the outgoing mail."

Using her handkerchief, Natalie took the note from him and carefully unfolded it. She didn't want to get any more fingerprints on it than there already were.

There was a single line typed in the middle of the page: *One down, many to go.*

The words had been typed by a laser printer, and she was willing to bet a year's salary that once the LVPD lab tech finished analyzing it, he would find nothing remarkable about the paper or the printer that had been used.

"We're all in danger, Natalie," her father repeated insistently.

She folded the note. Leaving it within the folds of her handkerchief, she placed it in her purse. She didn't have time to hold her father's hand—she had a murderer to track down.

"Try to think positive for once, Dad," she advised crisply. "I'll get back to you when I have more information," she said by way of parting.

She left him the way she found him, sitting on the terrace, staring off into space.

Though she did her best to talk herself out of it, Natalie could feel the adrenaline rush through her veins as she left the Rothchild grounds and made her way to The Janus.

It was coming in waves, she realized, a little like when she knew there was going to be a showdown. One that might leave her wounded.

There were few things in her life that Natalie had believed to be a certainty, but one of them was that she'd thought she would never see Matt Schaffer again. Eight years ago he'd vanished out of her life, leaving behind a one-line note tucked under a pillow that had grown cold. All the note had said was: *I'm sorry, but this just isn't going to work.*

That was it. No explanation, no real indication of remorse, no mention of the possibility that whatever it was that was taking him away from her could, in time, be resolved. The note had been as clinical, as removed and compassionless as an eviction notice, which, in effect, it was, she thought as she navigated through the morning traffic. Matt had written the note to evict her from his life.

She'd spent the next two weeks crying, breaking down without warning as she walked down the street, talked on the phone or sat, staring at a meal she couldn't bring herself to eat.

Candace, she remembered with a bittersweet pang, had tried to get her to go clubbing in order to get her to forget about Matt.

She'd turned her twin down, but she *did* get her act together. If Matt didn't think enough of their relationship to try to get in contact with her, to try to make her understand why he'd changed so radically from lover to stranger, then the hell with him. He was dead to her, she resolved. And he'd remained that way.

Until twenty minutes ago.

The adrenaline in her veins kept mounting.

Natalie focused on her driving. Vegas in the daylight wasn't nearly as alluring as it was after dark. Like an aging woman best seen in soft lighting, Vegas's imperfections were all visible in the daylight. Natalie supposed that was why people like her sister didn't like to get up until well past noon. They lived for the night.

Except that Candace could no longer do that.

The thought brought a fresh, sharp ache with it.

"Damn it, Candy, what a waste," Natalie murmured under her breath, calling her sister by the nickname she hadn't used in years. "What an awful, awful waste."

Reaching her destination, she pulled up before The Janus. As she did so, Natalie saw one of the three valets currently on duty make a beeline for her vehicle.

The lanky young man was quick to hide the frown that had begun to curl his lips.

He was undoubtedly used to parking a higher class of vehicle, Natalie thought. Unlike her twin, she was determined not to touch any of the family fortune or the trust fund that her grandfather had set aside for them on the day they were born. Instead, she lived on and spent only what she earned. Perforce, that limited her lifestyle. The salary of an LVPD detective didn't stretch very far, restricting her to the basic necessities of life. Consequently, her automobile was a six-year-old Honda Accord, but it proved to be more reliable than most of the people she knew.

"Welcome to The Janus," the young attendant said cheerfully as he opened the driver's side door for her with a flourish.

"We'll see," she replied solemnly.

As he pulled away with her car, Natalie looked up at the casino's logo. Janus was the Roman god with two faces, one pointed toward the past, the other facing the future. It struck her as rather ironic, given what she was doing here, seeking out someone from her past in order to get answers so that the future could be settled.

The moment she entered the casino, the Vegas phenomena took hold.

It was like stepping into a world where time did not matter or even make an appearance. Though there were cameras everywhere, capturing and time-stamping every movement that was made by the casino's guests, there were no clocks displayed throughout the actual casino, no measurement of time passing in any form. All there was was a sense of "now."

The feeling of immortality was created out of this sort of fabric, Natalie thought.

Because, in her experience, she'd discovered that bartenders knew the inner workings of any establishment they worked for better than anyone else, Natalie made her way to the first bar she came across.

The bartender in attendance was a gregarious man who looked to be in his early forties. He had premature gray hair and a quick, sexy smile, which was probably one of the main reasons he'd been hired. That, and his dexterity when it came to mixing drinks. She noted that he had fast hands.

His name tag identified him as Kevin.

Moving to her end of the bar, Kevin asked, "What'll it be, pretty lady?"

Slipping her hand between the bottom of the glass and the bar, Natalie stopped him from placing it down. "Information." She saw a dubious look cross his brow. To counter that, she took out her badge. Granted she wasn't here in an official capacity, but "Kevin" didn't need to know that. "Were you on duty last night?"

Because there was no one else at the bar seeking his services, Kevin began to wipe the gleaming black surface, massaging it slowly. "You mean during the gala?"

"Yes."

The smile gracing his lips was a satisfied one. Last night had obviously been profitable for him, she figured. "I caught an extra shift."

She took out Candace's photograph and carefully placed it on the bar, turning it around so that he could look at it head-on. "Did you happen to see this woman there?"

The bartender glanced at the picture. Mild interest

turned to recognition. "You mean Candace Rothchild? Yeah, she was here, loud and brassy as always. But not for long," he added, looking rather disappointed. There was always a circus when Candace was around, Natalie thought. People came along for the entertainment. "The boss and she had at it, and then he had Schaffer 'escort' her out."

She latched on to the first part of his statement. "They argued?"

"Yeah."

"About?"

He shook his head. "Couldn't tell you. Too far away for anything but body language," he confessed.

"And Schaffer?" she repeated.

"He got her to leave."

She leaned in over the bar. "Tell me about him."

"Don't know much," the bartender admitted. "Just that his name's Matt Schaffer, and he's Montgomery's head of security for the casino. Boss flew him in from L.A., where he's head of security for Montgomery Enterprises."

There was no avoiding it, she thought darkly. She was going to have to talk to Matt. The thought left her cold. "Do you know where I can find him right now?"

Kevin glanced at his watch. "He should be in his office."

She rarely frequented casinos, and when she did, they weren't ones that belonged to her father's rivals. Luke Montgomery had made no secret that he wanted to be the King of Vegas, a position that her father had once aspired to.

"And his office would be—?" She waited for the bartender to enlighten her.

"On the second floor, toward the rear." He pointed her in the right direction.

Taking out a twenty, she placed it on the bar. "Thanks for your help."

In a practiced, fluid motion, Kevin slipped the bill into his vest pocket. "Any time, lovely lady," he called after her. "Any time."

She debated going up the stairs, then decided on the elevator. The car that took her up to the second floor was empty. Natalie stepped out of the elevator, looked around to get her bearings and then walked toward the rear of the floor.

The office where the monitors and the people who watched them were housed was encased in dark, tinted glass walls. It gave her an opportunity to scan the room and its occupants before she entered.

None of them were Matt. But then, as head of security, he'd probably have his own area, she thought, most likely removed from the others.

Into the Valley of Death rode the six hundred, she silently recited, digging deep for a line from a poem by Tennyson. Wrapping her hand around the brass handle, she opened one of the glass doors and walked in.

The woman whose desk was closest to the door looked up and then began to cross to her. "I'm sorry, but you can't come in here. This is a restricted area."

Natalie already had her ID in her hand and held it up. "I'm looking for Matt Schaffer," she told the woman.

God, even saying his name made her mouth go dry. She was supposed to be over him, had moved on with her life. What happened?

The woman began to answer her. "He's—"

"Right here."

The deep voice came from behind her. Natalie felt every single nerve ending go on tactical alert at the same moment that all the hairs at the back of her neck stood up.

Despite the fact that it had been eight years, she would have recognized his voice anywhere.

"What can I...do for you?" The break in the question came because she turned around in the middle of his inquiry.

Natalie.

For a fraction of a heartbeat, Matt Schaffer stopped breathing. He'd known that, most likely, it would be just a matter of time before their paths crossed. Knew when he had reluctantly agreed to Luke Montgomery's proposition that he transfer to Vegas to oversee security at The Janus because there'd been a problem with the last man who'd been in charge. His only condition had been that the transfer be temporary, lasting only until someone reliable could be found to fill the slot.

If luck had been with him, he might have been able to avoid this.

But deep down in his bones, he'd known all along that this was destined to happen. Maybe even unconsciously he'd actually wished that it would. Now that it had, that same old feeling he'd always had around Natalie slipped over him.

If anything, Natalie had gotten more beautiful, not less. Her straight brown hair was still lustrous, still silky, and her eyes were that incredible shade of blue that could pull him in without warning. Maturity sat well on her, like a rosebud that had bloomed into a breathtaking flower. He felt that old magic, that crackle of chemistry humming between them.

The reasons he had walked away from her all those years ago were still valid, still in play. Leaving hadn't been a mistake. He'd done it for her, but God, he'd missed her all these years. So much so that it almost hurt to look at her. To look at her and realize all that he had missed. All that he would continue to miss, because nothing had changed.

"Natalie." He said her name warmly.

She raised her chin in that way he'd always found both endearing and amusing. More than once he'd wanted to give in to impulse and just nibble on it. He'd refrained, knowing the action would have earned him an indignant right cross because when she raised her chin like that, she wanted to be taken seriously. It was her tell, he thought, a sign that gamblers looked for in other gamblers because it was used to clue them in on what was to come next.

"Hello, Matt." Her voice was formal, devoid of any emotion, her body almost rigid. He could remember how fluid she felt in his arms. It made him ache. "It's been a long time."

And he'd been acutely aware of every moment of that passage of time without her. More than once he had thought about the way things could have been, if he had only been able to go back and change things, be someone different...

But he'd always come to the same conclusion—that it was useless to waste time wishing. Things were the way they were and that was that.

"Yes, it has," he agreed quietly. "What can I do for you?"

She made it cut and dried. All she wanted was to get this over with. "You can answer some questions and give me access to all of last night's surveillance tapes."

Whatever he was expecting, it wasn't this. "I don't understand—"

It was then that Natalie took out her badge again and held it up for him to look at. When they'd last been together, she'd just graduated college. Being a police-woman hadn't even entered her mind. All she wanted to do was spend her days and nights loving Matt. Just showed how naive and stupid the very young could be, she thought cynically.

"Candace Rothchild was here last night," she told him crisply.

"Yes, she was." Was this about his making her sister leave?

"She was also found dead in her condo early this morning. Time of death was sometime last night."

He stared at her, trying to process what she was telling him. "Your sister's dead?" he asked incredulously.

"Yes." The answer came out in a hiss between her teeth. Their paths hardly ever intersected anymore, but it was hard imagining a world without Candace in it. There'd be no more promises to make in fleeting moments of remorse only to break again the very next day. No more publicity-fraught attempts at trying to be a better mother to Mick and David. All that was gone now.

"I'm sorry for your loss, Natalie."

"Thanks." The single word was said without any emotion.

She saw the look of concern that came over his face. He'd become an accomplished actor since she'd last seen him, she thought cynically. One would have even thought he cared—except that she knew better. The only one Matt cared about was himself.

"Let's go to my office," he said in a low voice, turning on his heel to lead the way.

She had no choice but to follow.

Chapter 4

The moment Matt pushed the door open and walked into his spacious glass-enclosed office, the phone on his desk began ringing.

Talk about timing. An exasperated sound escaped his lips, and he looked over his shoulder at Natalie. "Do you mind if I get that?"

She gestured toward the multilined console on his desk. "Go ahead."

His being on the phone would give her a few more seconds to pull herself together, she thought. She hadn't realized seeing him again would affect her like this, shaking her to the core. If anything, his physique seemed more buff, harder, somehow. And looking into his blue eyes had her reliving bits and pieces of the past that made her feel so vulnerable. So much for being over him.

"Schaffer," Matt said as he put the receiver to his ear.

Natalie caught the shadow of a frown forming on his lips just before he turned his back to her. Matt lowered his voice, and even though she couldn't actually make out all the words, there was no missing the annoyed undercurrent.

"I don't have time for this, Scott," Matt finally said, cutting his older brother short on the other end of the line. He'd been in town less than two weeks and already Scott was seeking him out, dumping his problems in his lap. He wasn't about to allow himself to get sucked back into this kind of a rut again. He was done with all that. *Done.* "This time, you're going to have to bail yourself out of trouble."

The voice on the other end of the line begged indulgence.

Because this was his brother and because, God-only-knew-why but family still meant something to him despite all the turmoil it had caused in his life, Matt spared his older brother a minute more.

He sighed again, weary. "All right, I'll call you later. Until then, don't do anything stupid." Matt broke the connection before Scott could add another layer to the tale of woe that he'd been spinning.

Replacing the receiver in its cradle, Matt turned back around to look at Natalie. She looked stern, he thought. And beautiful despite her frown. "Sorry."

Her eyes met his. Hers were unfathomable. "Of course you are."

He would have had to have been deaf not to hear the sarcastic edge in her voice.

He had it coming, Matt thought, and he couldn't blame her, not after the way they had parted company. But he still felt in his heart that he had done the right thing.

Even if it hurt like hell at the time.

He wasn't exactly feeling terrific right now, he realized. Eight years and he still wanted her. Maybe even more than ever. He'd often wondered over the years, in isolated moments when he found himself alone, if he would ever get over her. He had his answer now. And it was a resounding "No."

She didn't need to know that, either, he thought, doing his best to appear impassive.

The next thing out of Natalie's mouth threw him for a loop.

"Did you have my sister killed?"

It took him a second to find his tongue. "What?" The implication behind the question had him reeling. How could she even *think* that? "Do you actually believe that I would be capable of something like that?"

Though she was certain that she gave no indication of it, she was struggling against her attraction to him. The fact that she could feel that, after all that had happened, disgusted her. She was supposed to be a stronger person than that. Right now, Natalie felt as if her emotions had been dumped into a blender, the button set on "high."

"I discovered a long time ago that I'm not exactly a great judge of character."

He had that coming, too, Matt thought. He refrained from commenting on her words. Instead, he answered her unsettling question.

"No, I didn't kill Candace." And then he hit her with a question of his own. "What could have possibly been my motive?"

She'd asked because her father had planted the idea

in her head, but she didn't want to bring him into the conversation just yet. "When they found her, Candace's ring was missing."

He stared at her, stunned. "Robbery?" he asked in disbelief. All right, his family had had some shady dealings in the past, but he himself had never been found guilty of anything. Had never traveled on the wrong side of the law. "You think I killed her to rob her?" Even as he said it, it sounded ludicrous. Matt looked at her for a long moment. "I don't believe you believe that," he told her quietly.

She didn't know what to believe. Her heart told her that Matt had nothing to do with this, but her heart hadn't exactly been batting a thousand.

"I really don't care what you believe," she informed him coldly. "The ring is worth millions. People do a lot of things for a lot less."

"People, maybe," he allowed. "But not me." And then the import of what she was saying hit him. "You're talking about the Tears of the Quetzal? *That* was the ring that was stolen?"

"As if you didn't know. Someone saw you escort Candace out."

They were attracting attention despite the closed door. Some of the people in the outer office kept glancing in their direction. Matt walked over to glass walls and one by one lowered the blinds, giving them privacy.

It also created a sense of intimacy that he really didn't want. Right now, it only complicated things. But he wanted prying eyes even less, so he left the blinds where they were. "A lot of people saw me escort Candace out."

"How far out?" Natalie challenged heatedly. "To

your car? Maybe you decided to take her for a little drive and wound up at her place?"

Candace and Natalie might have been twins but he had never met two sisters who were so utterly different, not just in looks but in personality. He had never experienced the slightest attraction, not even momentarily, to Candace.

"I walked her to the entrance," he told Natalie. "Where she went from there and with whom, I have no idea." She looked unconvinced. "I can show you the tape that verifies that." Although, he thought, he shouldn't have to.

"Tapes can be doctored," she countered. "As I remember, you were pretty good at that sort of thing. 'Enhancing' I think you called it."

That both wounded and irritated him, but he let it go. Instead, he appealed to her logic. Her logical mind was one of the things he'd loved about her.

"Natalie, think about it. What could I do with the ring if I did take it? I can't fence it. It's not some little piece of glitter. This rock is famous. Pieces have been written about it. A lot of people know what it looks like."

Everything Matt said made sense, but she wasn't willing to let him off the hook just yet. She needed more answers. "My father says he's into your family for a lot of money."

He was surprised her father had admitted that. Arrangements had been made secretly, so no one would know that Rothchild was in financial trouble.

"The family lent him money, yes."

Matt couldn't help thinking how ironic that was. Eight years ago, Harold Rothchild had come to him for the express purpose of buying him off. The man had offered him a quarter of a million dollars if he promised to disappear and never get in contact with Natalie again. Angry and offended because he knew that in Rothchild's eyes, he wasn't good enough for Natalie, he'd told her father what the man could do with his money and his offer.

And then, days later, his brother had succeeded in doing what Rothchild couldn't. He'd succeeded in making him leave Natalie, but for completely different reasons.

Natalie was looking at him suspiciously. They both knew what her father thought of the Schaffer family. "Why would your family give him a loan?"

Because Rothchild had told Natalie about the loan, he didn't feel bound by the initial promise of secrecy surrounding the deal. "Your father overextended himself. A note was due on his casino, and he stood to lose everything." He shrugged carelessly, his custom-made jacket rustling. "I was in a position to help." He'd been the one who had brokered the deal, acting as a go-between with his family and Rothchild.

That didn't answer her question. She pinned him with a look. "Again, why?"

He'd asked himself the same thing. This was a man who, eight years ago, would have gladly seen him run out of Vegas on a rail. But then he rethought his position. "Because he was your father, and I thought that what happened to him affected you. If he had to file for bankruptcy, your inheritance might be in jeopardy as well." He smiled at her. "Let's just say I thought I owed it to you."

Damn it, his smile wasn't supposed to affect her anymore, wasn't supposed to make her knees feel weak. She was a cop, for God's sake.

"You don't owe me anything, Schaffer," she told him, her voice edged with steel. "Except for straight answers."

"I gave you that," he told her. "I didn't kill Candace. I didn't *have* her killed, either," he added, covering all his bases. That, hopefully, out of the way, he had questions of his own. "How did she die?" he wanted to know.

She didn't answer him immediately. Instead, she looked at him for a long moment, debating whether or not she believed him. God help her, she did. Did that make her a fool?

After a beat, she decided there was no harm in answering. The papers would be carrying the story soon enough, and the media always had a way of ferreting things out.

"My guess is that the blow to the back of her head did it. And whoever was there got in a few licks on her face as well." Natalie shuddered. Had Candace suffered before she died? Lord, she hoped not. "Revenge, hatred, I don't know."

His eyes held hers. "And you thought I would do that?"

She gave him a nonanswer. "I had to ask."

He had a lot coming to him for the way things had ended between them, but not that. "No, you didn't."

Her temper flared. "Yes, I did," she insisted, struggling to keep her voice under control. "Because *I don't know you.*"

Yes, you do, Natalie. In your heart, you know me, he thought. And then another thought hit him. "Let me ask you a question."

"All right." Not knowing what to expect, she braced herself. "Ask."

He sat down on the edge of his desktop, crossing

his arms before him. "Have the rules changed since I left Vegas?"

He looked relaxed all of a sudden. Why? Where was he going with this? She became suspicious. "Depends on what kind of rules you're talking about."

He watched her expression as he spoke. "The rules that say a detective with a personal stake in a case isn't supposed to be allowed to investigate said case."

He should be the last one to talk about rules, she thought angrily. "No, they haven't changed," Natalie replied stoically.

Matt spread his hands in a silent question. "Well then, why—?"

She stopped him before he could go any further. "My captain put me on bereavement leave."

"That doesn't answer my question."

Well, not only did she not know him but he obviously didn't seem to know her, either she thought bitterly. "Do you honestly expect me to sit with my hands folded and not even *try* to find my sister's killer?" she snapped.

"No," he admitted, "I expect you to do exactly what you're doing. We have that in common, you and I." Their eyes met, and she wanted to look away, but found she couldn't. "We're both loyal to our families—even when they don't deserve it."

She took offense for her sister. "You're a fine one to pass judgment."

"I was talking about my own family," he clarified quietly, and with those few words, he effectively took the wind out of her sails.

"Oh." For a second, she was completely at a loss as to how to respond.

Sensing her discomfort, Matt changed the topic. He always had been in tune with her. "So, you're a police detective."

She looked at him warily. "Yes."

He smiled. It went straight to her belly. "Can't say that's something I saw in your future."

"I don't think there was anything you saw about my future." She couldn't refrain from making the dig. It kept her from demanding to know why he had walked out on her all those years ago without so much as a word of explanation.

There were so many things he wanted to say to her, but he didn't. They would all sound like excuses. And he knew she was better off this way. And safer. That had always been his goal, the motive behind his actions, to keep her as safe as possible. And that meant they couldn't be together. But if he'd told her the truth back then, she wouldn't have allowed it to keep them apart.

It was better this way. If he'd begun to waver in his decision, Scott's phone call had convinced him otherwise.

"I'd like to see those surveillance tapes from last night if you don't mind," she said crisply, her tone indicating that even if he did mind, she would still find a way to view them.

There were an awful lot of tapes to go through. They had a hundred different cameras just on the ground floor alone. That made for a great deal of viewing time. "What exactly is it that you're looking for?"

She wanted to say "anything suspicious" but she kept it succinct. "I want to see if Candace went home with anyone, or if anyone followed her."

There, at least, he could be of some help. "Well, I don't know for certain if anyone followed her, but I can tell you that when she left here, she was alone. I stood at the entrance and watched her for a few minutes to make sure she didn't double back."

He made Candace sound like some sort of undesirable. Granted her sister had been loud and tended to be outlandish at times, but she'd never been barred from any place. Casinos vied for her attendance.

"Exactly why was she escorted off the premises?"

"You'd have to take that up with Luke Montgomery," he told her.

His answer wasn't good enough. "You have no thoughts on that?" she wanted to know. "No impressions as to why he'd ask you to remove her?"

He told her what he knew. "They looked like they were quarreling when Montgomery signaled for me to come over."

The bartender had said the same thing. "Quarreling? Quarreling about what?" Maybe Montgomery sought Candace out later in her condo, to pick up in private where they had left off. She needed to know the nature of the argument.

Matt made an educated guess, based on what he knew about Candace. "I think your sister wanted to cause a sensation with her ring, and Montgomery wanted the focus to remain on the gems at the gala. Montgomery went to a lot of expense to get celebrities to donate the jewelry and get them all under one roof and, well, Candace always had a way of making love to the camera, to the exclusion of everyone else."

Natalie's eyes narrowed. "I guess you would know

about the lovemaking part." The retort was out before she could prevent its emergence.

She'd managed to catch him completely off guard. "Excuse me?"

Oh, he was good, Natalie thought. He really looked as if he didn't know what she was talking about. "Give it up, Matt. Candace told me that she thought you were really good in bed. One of her 'better' lovers, I believe she said."

For a moment, he was speechless. "Candace would have no way of knowing that."

She wasn't about to be taken in by his act, no matter how much part of her wanted to believe it. "Oh, don't bother playing innocent with me, Matt. Why would my sister lie?"

"The last thing I am is innocent," he informed her. "But I *never* made love to your sister and as for why she would lie to you, I could think of a dozen reasons. Her being a pathological liar would be at the top of the list." He saw that made Natalie angrier, but he stood by his statement. "I think, between her lifestyle, the booze, the drugs and the men, your sister lost her grasp on reality a long time ago."

Incensed, heartbroken and still in shock at seeing Matt after all this time, Natalie found herself in a very fragile state. Far more fragile than she ever thought she would be. Without thinking, she reacted, defending a sister who could no longer defend herself. She took a swing at Matt.

He caught her by the wrist, stopping her fist from making contact and then quickly caught the other when she switched hands.

Furious, she tried to pull free. "Let me go," she fumed.

"Only if you stop making a fist," he told her. When he saw her uncurl first one hand, then the other, he released her wrists.

And promptly received a stinging slap to his cheek. Without registering surprise—he really should have seen that coming, he upbraided himself—Matt merely looked at her as he rubbed his face.

"Feel better?"

She wanted to say yes, but nothing had been solved, nothing had been released. She still felt this pent-up anger, and it had nowhere to go. "No."

"I didn't think so." He wanted to take her hands in his, not to restrain her, but to make contact. He refrained, relying on his words instead to bridge the gap. "Look, I'm sorry about Candace, but unless you want to be next, I think you should leave this alone and let someone else handle it."

"Is that a threat?"

"That's an observation. Maybe the ring was just icing on the cake. You said she had bruises on her face. She didn't when she left here. Whoever killed your sister might have done so in a blind rage. Maybe revenge, not theft, was the motive."

"Revenge?" Natalie echoed. Candace had been thoughtless and had rubbed a great many people the wrong way, but she was harmless. She'd never done anything to anyone that would make them want to kill her. "You think whoever killed her was trying to teach her a lesson?"

He had a somewhat different theory to back up his thought. "No, maybe they were trying to get back at your father."

"My father?" she repeated. "Why?" But even as she asked, it made sense—if she thought of the note he'd shown her.

"All rich men make enemies along the way. What better way to get back at him than to kill someone in his family? One of his beloved daughters?"

She was still trying to turn this around on him. "You sound as if you're familiar with that kind of a life."

"Just speculating," he replied. "And if I'm right, you could be in danger."

"I'm a cop," she reminded him, deliberately resting her hand on the hilt of the weapon that was exposed beneath her jacket. "Being in danger kind of goes with the territory."

God help him but he suddenly had a very real urge to see her wearing her holster and a pair of stiletto heels—and nothing else.

"The territory," he advised, "might just have gotten a little rougher. I don't want anything happening to you."

If she could believe that...

But she couldn't. She knew better. "You have nothing to say about that," she informed him tersely. "You lost the right to have a say a long time ago, remember?"

He exhaled. It didn't help, didn't make the ache in his chest go away. "Yeah, I remember."

Chapter 5

"You know I can't release the tapes to you without a court order," Matt told her. There was protocol to follow, and even if things hadn't ended the way they did between them, technically his hands were tied. "And I'm guessing," he went on, "you can't get one because this isn't your case."

Her temper flared quickly, and it took effort to bank it down. She might have known he'd stonewall her. *Did* he have something to hide?

Natalie narrowed her eyes. She was not in the mood to be waved away like some annoying insect. "Look, Schaffer—"

Schaffer. She was calling him by his last name, the way a law enforcement agent would, he thought. The chasm between them was widening.

Good for her, he thought. She was moving on, or had moved on.

Bad for him, of course, but he'd resigned himself eight years ago that this was the way things had to be. Her father had been right all those years ago—he wasn't good enough for Natalie. Not because he didn't love her more than anything in the world but because his family would, in the end, drag him down. And if she were with him, they'd drag her down, too. He couldn't have that happen.

"However," he continued as if she hadn't interrupted him, "there really is nothing to stop you from looking over my shoulder as I review the tapes."

That stopped her in her tracks. "You're going to review the tapes?"

She couldn't read his expression. "The only responsible thing for a good citizen to do, don't you think?"

Natalie was surprised when a tinge of amusement whispered through her. "Is that what you are, a good citizen?"

"I do my best. Come with me," he said as he opened his office door.

The moment he did, there was a quick shuffling of bodies and rustling of chairs moving back into place. The techs in the surveillance room were returning to their posts, he thought. No doubt curiosity had gotten the better of them, with more than a few of the people who manned the monitors trying to get closer to his office in order to hear what was being said. Despite the fact that he was head of security for Montgomery Enterprises, he was, in effect, the "new kid on the block," at least in this location.

Until two weeks ago, he'd been based in Los Angeles, where he would have rather remained. But Montgomery had been adamant that he wanted him at The Janus, and the man did pay a damn good salary. Too good to refuse.

Making no comment about the temporary break that had been taken, Matt walked over to the computer tech seated just outside his office.

"Wilson—it is Wilson, right?" he asked the tall, painfully skinny, barely-out-of-adolescence young man.

Surprised at being singled out and obviously somewhat nervous because of it, the young man bobbed his head up and down. "Yes sir, Stuart Wilson."

Matt could see Wilson's Adam's apple moving up and down like a runaway golf ball. He'd looked into all their backgrounds his first day here. Wilson was the best of the best when it came to computers. What he couldn't make a computer do *couldn't* be done.

But the young technician's considerable proficiency didn't make him any less gawky, Matt thought. Wilson really needed to have someone take him under their wing, he mused.

Too bad he wasn't going to be here long enough for that. Matt had already made up his mind that he was going to be in Vegas just long enough to give The Janus's security system a once-over and babysit it until Montgomery hired a suitable replacement for him.

"Wilson, I need you to pull up the surveillance tapes that we have of Mr. Montgomery's gala last night."

Wilson's mouth dropped open as his jaw slackened. His small eyes widened as far as they could go. "All of them?" he repeated, stunned. Nervously, he added, "That's an awful lot of footage, sir."

He should have been more specific, Matt thought.

"Let's start with what we have between eight and nine o'clock. For the time being, I'm only interested in the first floor." He narrowed it down even more. "Make it the entrance and the casino floor between that and Ballrooms B and C."

The two ballrooms had been combined for the evening in order to accommodate all the people who had RSVPed that they were attending. By the middle of the evening, the two rooms were teeming with celebrities. He knew that Montgomery had pulled in a sizable amount for the charity he was sponsoring. In addition he had earned himself a great deal of goodwill and thereby excellent publicity, which he knew had been Montgomery's underlying goal.

Right now, the man was golden, Matt mused. Luke Montgomery had come a long way from the poor boy who'd been ridiculed for wearing the same clothes to school day after day. And, to his vast credit, Montgomery had risen far above his poverty-stricken roots without resorting to any deals with the devil.

In this case, Matt thought, that would be the other members of his family, from whom he would have enjoyed maintaining a continuing estrangement. However, his brother kept insisting on calling him, asking for help. It wasn't in him to say no.

He was working on that.

Wilson's long, thin fingers were flying across the keyboard. The resulting staccato rhythm, coming fast and furious, sounded not unlike rapid gunfire from a small handgun.

As Natalie watched the technician's monitor, the first of many tapes began to play across the screen. "Here's the tape of the entrance," Wilson announced.

Matt nodded. He rethought his offer to Natalie about having her look over his shoulder. He had things to attend to, and if he wound up spending any length of time sitting so close to her, well, he'd just rather not put himself to that sort of test.

Turning to Natalie, he indicated a nearby empty desk. One of the computer techs had called in sick this morning.

"Why don't you pull up a chair beside Wilson?" he suggested. "He'll be able to go through all the pertinent tapes for you."

Wilson stopped typing, anxiously darting his eyes between the two of them. "Is there anything specific that you're looking for?" he asked Natalie nervously.

It was easy to see that the tech was far more comfortable with computers than he was with people, Natalie thought. She pulled the chair over from the other desk and sat down beside Wilson, then took out the photograph she had of Candace and placed it beside the keyboard.

"I'm looking for any footage you have of this woman." She looked at the tech's face, expecting to see some sort of indication that he recognized her sister. Candace had attended every wild party, frequented all the casinos and in general had done her level best to turn herself into a household name.

Candace, Natalie couldn't help thinking, would have been bitterly disappointed with Wilson. There was absolutely no sign of recognition. He merely nodded at what he took to be his assignment. "Okay, let's see if I can find her."

As the tech began typing again, Matt withdrew. Natalie was aware the exact second that he stepped away and went back to his office.

Damn it, eight years and her Matt-radar was as keen as ever. The very *air* seemed to change when he was close by.

Get a grip, she sternly reminded herself. *You're here to find Candace's killer, not reignite something that was doomed from the beginning.*

With concentrated effort, Natalie settled in and focused on the images that were going by on Wilson's screen.

More than an hour had passed. Her neck was getting stiff, and she felt as if she was going to go cross-eyed. Tape after tape had been accessed and screened. A lot of the "beautiful people" came and went, each and every one of them had been greeted by Montgomery with enthusiasm.

The man certainly looked the part of a casino mogul, she couldn't help thinking. It was almost as if he'd been sent over from Central Casting. Suave, six foot two, muscular, dark-haired and handsome.

Almost as handsome as Matt.

Where the hell had that come from? she silently lamented. Looks weren't everything. As a matter of fact, looks were nothing, absolutely nothing if there was no heart. She'd learned that the hard way, thanks to Matt Schaffer.

Her mind wandering, she was suddenly jolted back to the present. Alert, she straightened in her seat. "Wait, go back," she ordered Wilson.

The tech jumped in surprise. Quickly, he rewound the footage.

"Stop!"

"This her?" he wanted to know. He'd just accessed footage from the front of the casino. The time stamp on the tape was 8:47 p.m. A sultry Candace, her scarlet gown clinging to her curves with every step she took, filled the monitor. Natalie thought she heard Wilson murmur an appreciative, "Wow."

That was the best word to use when summing up Candace, Natalie thought. *Wow*.

As she watched her sister walk down the red carpet, she felt a lump suddenly forming in her throat. Her eyes were moistening.

Damn it, where were all these stampeding emotions coming from?

She usually had better control over herself than this. But then, she supposed in her own defense, she wasn't usually confronting videos of a slain family member while sitting in the office of a former lover who had turned her heart into Swiss cheese.

Blowing out a breath, Natalie forced herself to watch the screen and analyze what she saw. This was no time to give in to tears.

From all indications, Candace appeared to be alone. And then, as Natalie watched, her sister's face lit up as if she saw someone she knew. Not unusual in a town that her sister had regarded as her personal playground, Natalie mused wryly. Whoever she spotted was off camera, part of the reporters elbowing each other out of the way for an outstanding shot.

As she continued to view the tape, she saw Candace begin to head directly over toward Montgomery.

Unlike his gracious behavior toward all the other attendees, the casino owner actually looked annoyed to see Candace. There wasn't even the pretense of cordiality, she noted.

Candace, on the other hand, looked delighted to see him. She was animated, and with every word she uttered, she would wave her left hand around. It was almost as if she was attempting to cast a spell.

Natalie slid to the edge of her chair. "Can you pull in on that?" she asked Wilson. "On her hand," she specified when he looked at her quizzically.

"Sure." The next moment, her left hand had all but filled the entire screen.

Natalie blinked. The image was somewhat grainy, but unmistakable. Her father was right. Candace had taken the ring, and she'd had it on when she walked into the casino. But not when they found her body in the condo.

Was the motive just robbery? Then why leave the necklace?

And just how had Candace gotten her hands on the ring in the first place? She would have bet anything that her father was the only one with the combination to the safe. He didn't trust anyone else with it. But then, maybe the ring hadn't been in the safe in the first place. Maybe her father had only alluded to it being there to throw everyone in the family off.

Maybe that eye candy he'd married had given him cause for concern and he'd moved the ring. Without realizing that Candace had observed him.

It was all just pure speculation. She needed facts. Fact, Candace had the ring on at 8:47 p.m. Fact, she didn't when they found her body the next morning. *This* morning, she thought grimly. *What was I doing while you were fighting for your life, Candy? Was I sleeping? Watching that old movie on TV?* She couldn't even remember the title.

A pervasive feeling of deep sorrow filled her.

Wilson, she noted, was waiting for her to tell him what to do.

She waved him on. "Okay, go back to the regular image," she requested.

When he did, she instructed him to keep going and then watched in silence as an obvious argument erupted between her sister and Montgomery. It escalated quickly. Within a few minutes, the casino owner gave up trying to reason with Candace and was signaling to someone.

Natalie didn't need to guess who. She pressed her lips together as she watched Matt come on the scene. Very politely, he took hold of Candace's arm.

Her stomach churned as she saw her sister turn up her charm. She was obviously playing up to Matt. Had she been right after all? Had there been something between the two of them?

There'd been rumors circulating that he had been one of Candace's lovers. There'd even been some talk that he had fathered one of her sons. Given the boys' ages, that would have meant that he had returned to Vegas, at least for a little while, six years ago. It didn't make any sense.

Trying to sort through her feelings, Natalie's head began to ache. She didn't know what to believe. All she knew was that she'd never felt as alone—and lonely—as she did right at this very moment.

Her hand to her forehead, she went on watching. Matt brought her sister to the casino's front entrance, just as he had told her that he had. And, also as he had said, he then stood there for several minutes, looking out. Presumably watching Candace walk away and making sure that she didn't attempt to come back.

All right, from all appearances, Candace left the casino. Did she hook up with someone just outside? Or did someone, captivated by that damn ring she kept sticking in people's faces, follow her home? All these questions nagged at her. She needed answers.

"Can we get a shot of the outside of the casino?" she asked Wilson.

He hesitated. "I'd have to access the footage from the valet area," he explained.

She didn't want excuses. "Just do it," she instructed.

"Yes'm," Wilson mumbled into his disappearing chin. Again, his fingers flew across the keyboard almost like independent digits. They seemed to be going at just under the speed of light. Natalie could feel her impatience mounting as the tempo increased.

And then Wilson accomplished his goal. He got the right footage. Candace was seen from another angle, this time from the outside of the building. She was moving away from the entrance.

She was pouting like a child who had been refused the toy she desired. And then, just like that, her face lit up again.

A beat later, she'd moved offscreen.

Natalie half rose in her seat. "Where is she going?" she demanded. When Wilson didn't answer her, she looked at the computer technician expectantly. "Get me the tape from the next camera." To clarify, she pointed at the screen. "The one to the right of this one."

"I—I can't," Wilson stuttered.

"What do you mean, you can't?"

The tech looked completely intimidated. "I—I would if I—I could, ma'am, but that one is—is down." As he spoke, his stutter became more pronounced.

God, now she was scaring geeky technicians, Natalie thought, feeling guilty.

She took a breath, then released it, trying her best to sound less threatening. Inside, she was tied up in knots. She was *certain* that whoever killed her sister was just offscreen.

"What do you mean it's down?"

"As in not working," Matt told her easily, coming up behind her chair. She swung around to face him. "It happens."

She didn't believe in coincidences. Someone had put that camera out of commission. "Conveniently," she bit off.

Matt moved so that his back was to the computer and he could see her better. "As a matter of fact, very inconveniently."

All right, whoever Candace had seen wasn't on camera. But that didn't mean she couldn't find out who it was. "I want to talk to all the valets who were parking cars last night," she told him.

Matt inclined his head. "That can be arranged," he told her. And then he smiled at her and said, "Ask me nicely."

She gritted her teeth together. Maybe this was entertaining him, but she meant business.

"I want to talk to the valets who were parking cars last night or you're going to suddenly find yourself a guest of the city for impeding a homicide investigation." She shot him a warning look. "And I promise you, Schaffer, you really won't like the accommodations."

He crossed his arms before him. "That wasn't asking nicely, Natalie," he observed.

She jumped up to her feet. "Look—" But she got no further.

Because, just then, Adam Parker and Miles Davidson pushed open the door and walked into the surveillance room.

Both men looked as surprised to see her as she was to see them.

Parker frowned at her. "You wouldn't be conducting an investigation into your sister's death after the captain gave you explicit orders not to and put you on bereavement leave, would you Rothchild?" he asked.

Natalie didn't know if the question was tongue in cheek or not. She was pretty certain the men would turn a blind eye to her pursuing leads as long as it wasn't right in front of them. This put all three of them in an awkward position.

"As a matter of fact, Natalie's here visiting me," Matt informed the detectives genially. Both men looked rather dubious. "We used to be close," he went on. "I invited her in here so that I could keep an eye on the monitors while we caught up on old times." As he talked, he approached the detectives. Passing Wilson's desk, Matt pressed a key on the board so swiftly that the movement was all but imperceptible.

Except that Natalie saw him.

A long, narrow bar appeared on the bottom of the screen, indicating that something was currently being saved.

Matt deliberately placed his body before the two detectives and in front of Wilson's computer, effectively blocking it.

He looked from one man to the other. "I'm Matt Schaffer, head of Montgomery Enterprises security." He shook each detective's hand in turn. "Is there anything I can do for you?"

"Yeah." Parker nodded toward the computers in general. "You can hand over all your surveillance tapes from last night."

Matt remained unfazed. "That's a tall order, detective. Do you have a subpoena?"

Parker reached into his inside pocket and took out an envelope. "Right here."

Natalie felt her heart sink.

Chapter 6

He smiled to himself as he watched the news on the flat-panel TV in his dreary apartment. Another building blocked sunlight from entering through the window, but that didn't dampen his spirits. Today, he felt on top of the world.

Didn't take long, did it? he thought, tossing away the greasy wrapper that had held his fast-food lunch. But then, the media was full of nothing but sharks these days no matter what venue they reported in. The moment they smelled blood—in this case, a story about a tabloid queen who'd led an in-your-face life since she put on her first pair of thong underwear—there was a feeding frenzy.

The story had broke early this morning, and there'd been nothing but a recycling of details, ad nauseam, since then.

No matter, it would be a long time before he got tired of hearing them.

"There'll be more to join her soon enough," he promised the attractive blonde whose turn it was to interrupt the scheduled morning programming with this "Breaking news."

A wicked smile curved his mouth, marring his handsome features. One by one, he was going to make all the Rothchilds pay for what had been done, both to his father and, consequently, to his mother.

"Think he can clear his conscience by throwing a few dollars our way?" he seethed, addressing the words to the air. "Was that supposed to make up for robbing us of Poppi *and* what was his? Well, Rothchild's in for one hell of a surprise if that's what he thinks."

The laugh that echoed within the dim room sounded more like a demonic giggle.

He slipped his hand into his pocket and curled his fingers around the prize he'd secured last night. It comforted him not because of what it was but because he knew that Harold Rothchild grieved over its absence probably even more than he grieved for his daughter's demise. The newscaster was saying something about robbery being the motive.

Let them think that, he thought. Stealing the dazzling ring had just been the cherry on top of the sundae. Hitting Rothchild where it hurt most. Besides, he wasn't stealing; he was reclaiming. The gem belonged to his family, not Rothchild's. And his aim was to go on eliminating family members until old man Rothchild was the last man standing.

Once Rothchild's entire family was gone, then and

only then, would he move in to bring an end to the old man's misery. Slowly, he decided. Very, very slowly. He was going to enjoy hearing Rothchild beg for mercy.

His father had never had the chance, he thought bitterly. Joseph Rothchild had been his father's judge and executioner—and Harold Rothchild had stood in the shadows and watched, shaking like a little girl, too afraid of his own father to do the right thing and intervene.

Well, this was going to teach that spineless bastard to mess with his family, the young man promised himself with mounting glee.

Knowing he needed to go out, he looked around the small, airless apartment, searching for a place to leave the priceless ring. But there was nowhere within the three untidy rooms that he, as an accomplished thief, wouldn't have looked in his search for goods. Thieves were rampant in this city of glitter and sin.

The safest place, for now, he decided, was with him. So he left it in his pocket.

His smile widened. It was the kind of malevolent look that made a man's blood run cold, he thought proudly, catching a glimpse of himself in the cracked, smoky mirror that he passed on his way to the door.

Besides, in the right hands, the hands of the family who were the rightful owners of the diamond, wasn't it supposed to bring some kind of good luck? Since his father had been the one to have originally found the gem in that godforsaken mine, that meant the multicolored diamond with its hypnotic gleam belonged to *his* family. And that, in turn, meant that it was supposed to bring *him* luck.

In a way, he mused philosophically, it already had.

He'd killed Candace Rothchild and no one was the wiser. No one had seen it coming, not even Candace until the late few moments. The lying, empty-headed bitch thought she was going to have a blood-pumping roll in the sack, not receive a one-way ticket for a trip on the River Styx.

Surprise!

Curling his fingers around the ring, he walked out of his apartment whistling. He took care to lock the door behind him.

Natalie watched in silence as the two men she worked with cleared out the last of the surveillance tapes. They packed the lot of them into a box that one of Matt's people had provided. Parker had the decency to look contrite as the other detective hefted the box.

"Sorry, Nat," the older man apologized, and then he paused because he didn't want working relations to deteriorate between them. "But we'll get him—or her," he augmented since the killer had left no indication as to gender. There was always an outside chance that Candace had been done in by a jealous wife or girlfriend who had been thrown over by her man because the partying heiress had come on the scene.

Natalie sighed and nodded her head. It was clear to Matt that passive was not a role she played well. He waited until the two detectives had left with their booty, then looked expectantly at the young technician. Without a word, Wilson began typing, his fingers flying again.

Natalie had caught the look that had gone between the two. Caught, too, the swift sleight of hand that had occurred when Matt had passed the technician's keyboard. She doubted if either Parker or Davidson had noticed. If they had, something would have been said. Matt was still that good.

"What did you do?" she asked him.

His intensely blue eyes looked at her with amusement. "Excuse me?"

There was a time when she would have found this charming. But that naive girl had grown up years ago.

"Don't try to sound innocent, Schaffer. It's far too late for that. When Parker and Davidson came in, before they even asked you for the tapes, you did something on the keyboard as you walked by. Don't bother denying it," she cautioned. "I saw you."

"My hand slipped," Matt deadpanned. He knew that it was just a matter of seconds before the computer was finished going through its paces and he had what he needed.

Who the hell did he think he was kidding? Natalie thought.

"That might fly with Parker. He doesn't know computers—or you—the way I do." Her eyes narrowed, pinning him. "Now, what did you do?"

He would have thought she would have figured it out by now. "I backed up the tapes that were just handed over to your buddies."

Even though she'd viewed the pertinent ones, she'd still wanted to have the tapes so that she could look them over more closely. She looked at him in surprise. "You made me a copy?"

"I made *me* a copy," he corrected, then added loftily. "And, if you're very nice to me, I just might let you have them—"

She was not in the mood to play games—and even if she was, it wouldn't have been with him. "You're obstructing justice—" she began.

"On the contrary," he contradicted her in a mild, easygoing voice that she found infinitely irritating. "I cooperated with law enforcement. Law enforcement just took the tapes with them. You, in this case, are a private citizen, remember?"

She pinned him with a look. "I also have a temper, remember?"

Matt grinned then, recalling how volatile she could be—and how much fun making up afterward always was. It was hard to believe that he had once been that young, that devoid of a sense of impeding consequences to have considered allowing her to remain in his life. He knew better now.

"How could I forget it?" And then he added, "Don't worry, I still remember how to share and play well with others." He looked toward the tech. "Are you finished?"

"Just about." Wilson pushed his glasses up his noise, something she noticed he did every few minutes. "Just gotta put it on a disk."

"Make it a jump drive," Matt told him. He took what looked like a key chain advertising Montgomery Enterprises out of his pocket and handed it to the tech. "Easier to carry around." He said the words to the tech, but he was pointedly looking at Natalie as he said them.

He was going for "hide in plain sight," she thought. "Thank you," she said grudgingly.

Matt was already walking away, and he shrugged in response. "I owe you."

Natalie saw no reason to dispute that. "Yes," she agreed emphatically. "You do."

Three minutes later, the newly uploaded key chain in hand, she walked into Matt's office without bothering to knock first. There was a TV on the side of the office, and he had it on, giving it his attention for the moment. But he was aware of her entrance. She still wore the same fragrance.

Matt turned around in his chair. "Leaving now?" he asked.

She was about to say no, but the words temporarily evaporated from her lips. Her eyes were drawn to the TV on the back wall despite the fact that he had the sound lowered. Along the bottom of the screen was a banner announcing "Breaking news." Candace's photograph, taken at some other recent function, was in the upper right-hand corner as a newscaster read words off a teleprompter announcing to the few who hadn't yet heard that Candace Rothchild, the darling of the paparazzi set, had been found dead in her condo. Because the room where she was found had been ransacked, the banner continued, foul play was suspected.

"Foul play," Natalie echoed incredulously, spitting the term out. "What an innocuous term for murder."

He was well aware that news reporting was an art form. They had to tantalize the public, taking care not to put them off so much that they couldn't bear to hear the details.

"Keeps the public coming back for more and still separates them from the horror of it." Something protective kicked in within him. Leaning over, he deliberately turned off the TV. She didn't need to be subjected to that.

"Otherwise, if you showed all the gruesome details, the only ones who'd tune in would be serial killers in the making. And ghouls," he added. He rose from his desk, guessing why she'd sought him out. "Leaving?"

Natalie shook her head. "Just getting started," she contradicted.

He'd forgotten how stubborn she could be. Like a junkyard dog once she got hold of something—except a lot prettier. Still, he knew he had to give appealing to her common sense a shot. "Natalie, I really think you should leave this to the others."

Was he serious? "And I really think you should help me."

He thought that his part was over with the tapes. "What?"

Damn, she hated sounding as if she was asking for favors, but he was right. She had no official capacity here, couldn't rely on her badge, so this placed it in the realm of favors.

"Believe me, this is not something I'm asking lightly, but you were the last one to see Candace alive," she reminded him.

"Correction, a whole plaza full of people were the last ones to see your sister alive—not to mention whoever killed her," he added.

She intended on asking questions until someone remembered something, or said something that would point her in the right direction. For that, she needed him, because he could pave the way for her. And, as he had already mentioned, he owed her.

"I need to talk to Luke to find out what the argument was about, and I need to talk to the valets on duty to see if any of them noticed anyone leaving with Candace," Natalie told him. "She was obviously smiling at *someone* off camera."

As she paused, she realized that Matt looked as if he was going to refuse her. She wasn't about to give him the chance. She intended on hammering at him until he surrendered.

"Now, I'm going to do this with you or without you," she said, "but it would go a whole lot easier for me if you were there to smooth the way for me."

"Natalie—"

He still looked dubious. Did having her around repulse him so much that he would deny her the right to find her sister's killer?

She guessed at the reason behind his reluctance. It had been eight years. She hadn't expected time to freeze for him—the way it had for her. "Don't worry. As soon as I have my answers, I'll be gone. You won't need to explain me to your wife or girlfriend or whatever."

"I'm not worried about that," he told her. She didn't realize how much of a hole her absence had left, but then, why should she? "And for the record, there's no wife or girlfriend or 'whatever.'"

He wasn't married, wasn't involved with anyone. Natalie could feel her heart do a little leap in her chest and she tried in vain to pay no attention to it.

"Good," she responded crisply, "then you're free to help."

He pointed out the obvious. "I'm working," but even as he said it, he knew it wasn't an excuse. She was determined, and he was afraid that she would push too hard and get herself killed as well.

"We're not going to Mars. We're staying on the premises." She frowned at him. "Now, are you going to help me?" She drew closer to him, as if her proximity would draw the words out of him. "Or do you have something to confess?"

Her scent filled his head, triggering memories. Nostalgia brought a side order of yearning with it.

Yes, I have something to confess. I never got over you. You're a fever in my blood, Natalie Rothchild. And seeing you now has just made me realize that I was a fool to ever think I could put you behind me.

But he kept all of this tightly wrapped inside of him. If he said anything at all, then he'd wasted the last eight years trying to make a life for himself without her. So he kept his face impassive and glanced at his watch. "I can give you an hour."

Eight years ago, he called the shots. This time around it was her turn. "You'll give me as much time as I need," she countered.

Amusement curved his lips. "You've gotten tougher since I last saw you."

Her eyes met his for a long moment. "I've had to," was all she said.

There had been five valets on duty last night. Because of the double duty they'd pulled, they were all off now and had to be summoned back to the casino.

"This is where your part comes in," Natalie told him as he had the head attendant place calls to all five valets. Matt made no comment as he gave the attendant instructions.

One by one, the valets—all young, lean men in their

twenties, came straggling in. They looked bleary-eyed and somewhat bewildered. The gala hadn't ended until two in the morning.

Natalie decided that questioning them en masse would be simpler. In response, she heard the same story over and over again. Between regular guests of the casino and its accompanying hotel, and the attendees at the gala, all five valets had been kept hopping. They were far too busy parking and retrieving cars to take any kind of notice of the comings and goings of the attending celebrities for more than a fleeting second, if that long.

What it boiled down to was that they all assured Natalie that they hadn't seen who Candace might have left with. Her optimism was flagging when the last valet suddenly remembered that he had seen the flamboyant young woman exchanging words with another woman.

"She didn't exactly look pleased," the valet confided to her.

She took a guess as to who the pronoun referred to. "Candace?"

The young man shook his head. "No, the woman Miss Rothchild was talking to."

Excitement instantly sparked. "Could you describe her?"

The valet, Blake, looked at her sheepishly. "No," he confessed. It took him a moment to continue. When he did, he avoided looking into Natalie's eyes. "I was watching Ms. Rothchild. She was um, gesturing so hard that, um…" And then, because he seemed to suddenly realize he was talking to the dead woman's sister, he abruptly stopped, red-faced.

It took no effort for Matt to read between the lines. "You were watching to see if her dress would stay put or fall off."

The words sounded antiseptic, but the valet still looked somewhat embarrassed by what he'd accidentally admitted to. Still, he seemed aware that she was waiting for him to answer. So he made the admission to his shoes. "Yeah, that's it."

Natalie couldn't begin to describe the frustration she felt. She grabbed hold of the valet's arm and tugged, forcing him to look up at her. "You have to remember *something*," she insisted. "Blonde? Brunette? Redhead? Tall? Short?"

The valet pressed his lips together and screwed his face up, hard. It looked as if he was straining his brain. Any second, Natalie was certain she was going to see steam coming out of his ears. Finally, he said, "She wasn't old."

"Great," Natalie murmured. "I'll put out an APB for half of Vegas."

The valet looked genuinely contrite. "Sorry," he apologized.

Matt put his hand on the young man's shoulder. "It's all right, Blake," he told him. "You can go back home now." Matt looked at the other valets still gathered there. "That goes for the rest of you—unless anyone remembers anything else."

"No."

"Sorry."

"Not me."

"It was a busy night, Mr. Schaffer."

Matt nodded. "I know. Get some sleep, you'll be back on duty soon."

The valets immediately cleared out, obviously relieved to be dismissed.

Natalie turned on Matt, her hands on her hips. He'd usurped her authority, just like that. "Maybe I wasn't finished with Blake," she said, struggling to rein in her irritation.

"What were you planning on doing?" he challenged. "Performing exploratory surgery on his brain to see if he was hiding something? The kid told you all that he remembered."

Something was nagging at her. In Natalie's opinion, Matt had been much too lax with the valets, almost eager to send them on their way—especially the last one. Was he covering for this Blake guy?

Or was he covering for someone else? She hated this feeling, but she just didn't trust him. "And have you told me all you know, or are you hiding something?"

He could only shake his head. How many times were they going to go through this? "I'm the one who called the valets in, remember? And the one who got you a backup of the tapes." He would have thought that the latter would have gotten him some goodwill. "When did you get so suspicious of everyone?"

There was no hesitation on her part. She fired back, "The day I found a note tucked under the pillow next to mine."

What could he say to that? That he had done it for her own good? That it had killed him to leave her? That he'd looked back at her sleeping face, so peaceful, so beautiful, and had almost changed his mind? That he had almost torn up the note and had wanted nothing more than to take his chances? Except that the chances he'd be taking didn't involve him, they'd involved her and he had no right to play Russian roulette with her life for the selfish reason that he couldn't live without her.

He'd learned how to.

Matt said nothing in response. Instead, he asked, "Do you still want to talk to Montgomery?"

"Yes."

He nodded. "Then let's go."

Chapter 7

The automatic smile that appeared on Luke Montgomery's lips as she entered his office, followed by Matt, faded instantly when Natalie confronted him with her first question.

It was obvious that Montgomery didn't like being questioned or put on the spot, especially not by an LVPD detective that also just happened to be the daughter of a man who had once scoffed at his efforts to get started in the casino business. Harold Rothchild's exact words had been that he would look forward to being a witness to his failure.

A man didn't forget words like that. They either crushed him or spurred him on. For Luke, it was the latter.

He absently wondered if the senior Rothchild knew that he was, at least in part, responsible for the influential man he had become. Nothing like wanting to prove someone wrong to make a man become driven.

"Am I under arrest, *detective?*" The casino mogul deliberately enunciated her title as if he were an adult humoring a child deeply entrenched in the world of make-believe.

Inwardly, Natalie bristled at his tone but kept it under wraps. She knew that a display of temper was what he was after.

"Would you be more inclined to answer my questions if you were?" she countered, a cool, polite smile on her lips. "Because if that's what it takes, we can do that dance and waste a lot of each other's time. You can call your lawyer, and he can come down and brief you as to what you can and can't say to me and I can hang around, waiting. *Or* we can act like mature adults and get on with it—" Her eyes pinned his. "I'm assuming, of course, that you have nothing to hide."

Luke fixed her with a look that would have made a person with less to lose nervously retreat. But Natalie was in this to win, to get answers about her sister, and she wasn't about to back down.

"You assume correctly. I have nothing to hide," he informed her in a voice that was completely devoid of any emotion.

We'll see about that, Natalie promised silently. "Great. So what was it that you and my sister argued about last night?"

"Who said we argued?" Montgomery wanted to know. The look he slanted toward Matt said that, as far as he was concerned, the question was rhetorical.

"A few of the people who attended the gala last night mentioned that you were less than pleased with

Candace and that you both raised your voices at one another," she told him.

Her response to Montgomery's question surprised Matt. He'd fully expected her to tell his boss that she'd gotten the information from him.

He smiled to himself. *Still full of surprises, aren't you, Natalie?*

For a moment, Luke said nothing, as if debating just how much he was willing to admit to. He might be flamboyant when out in public, but there was a part of him that was exceedingly private. The irony of wanting privacy and running a business in a town like this was not lost on him.

But, he decided, stubbornly refusing to answer Rothchild's question would be more trouble than it was worth.

"Your sister thought we could pick up where we left off. We couldn't," he ended simply. "That didn't make her very happy." It was an understatement, and they all knew it. Candace had been a drama queen from way back. "Neither did my telling her that she was taking the spotlight away from a very worthwhile charity, and I wasn't going to allow it."

Natalie nodded. Even though she hated to admit it, that sort of thing sounded exactly like something Candace would try to do—upstage a charity event. Sadly, her sister was that shallow.

"That sounds like Candace," she acknowledged with a sigh.

Montgomery rose from his desk, giving every indication that he intended to walk Natalie to the door. "So, are we done?" he demanded.

Natalie remained where she was. "Just one more question, Luke—you don't mind if I call you Luke, do you?" She didn't wait for an answer, but continued talking. "Where were you last night from the hours of eleven to three?"

The look in his eyes told her he really resented having to account for himself. When he answered, it was through clenched teeth. "The first part I was at the gala. Hundreds of people can vouch for that," he added crisply.

"And the second part of that time frame?" she prodded.

Luke's eyes darkened. "None of your business."

Oh, but it was, she thought. She felt Matt move closer to her. Was he going to back her up or draw her away? She didn't wait to find out. "This isn't for some blog, Luke. I'm asking as a homicide detective. Where did you go after you left the gala?"

Montgomery took offense at her line of questioning. "Then I *am* under suspicion?"

His voice had risen. She was determined to keep hers level. "*Everyone* is under suspicion until their alibi is checked out," she said.

And then, just like that, Montgomery relented. His voice became almost mild. "I was with a lady in her hotel room."

That was going to have to be verified, and they both knew it. "I'm assuming this 'lady' has a name." She waited for him to give it to her.

Montgomery shrugged. "Most likely. I don't happen to remember it."

Was he deliberately being vague—or was he lying? In either case, Natalie shook her head, her eyes never leaving his. "Not good enough."

"But I do remember the room number," Montgomery added after a beat.

It seemed to Natalie that he was intentionally playing some sort of a game, wording this so that she was led to assume that he might have had something to do with Candace's murder. The possibility had occurred to her. After all, it was no secret that Montgomery and her father were less than friendly rivals. She'd heard her father rant about the other man more than once, complaining bitterly that the latter was encroaching on territory that should have been his. It seemed as if the Rothchild fortunes were taking a downturn just as Montgomery's were on the upswing.

"Good," she ground out when he didn't immediately volunteer the number. "What was it?"

"Room 1312. Oh," he added innocently, "and she said something about having to get back to the East Coast by this evening so I'd hurry getting up there if you want to catch her to back up my 'alibi.'" Montgomery tossed the term at her with a smug satisfaction that told her he was either way overconfident—or he wasn't guilty of anything more than being arrogant.

"Thanks for the heads-up," she responded.

Natalie kept a poker face despite the wave of acute disappointment. It would have been gratifying to lay Candace's murder at Montgomery's doorstep. But that would have been far too easy, and she knew from experience that ninety-five percent of the time, the easy route never led to the right conclusion.

"Okay, I don't need you anymore," Natalie told Matt the moment they hit the lobby. She was striding toward the elevator banks. "You can go back to whatever it was you were doing."

He'd been a reluctant participant, but now that he was with her, Matt felt an even greater reluctance to pull away. "Thanks, but I think I'll stick around a little longer. You might find you need me."

"Not in a million years," she said a tad too vehemently.

Matt pretended not to hear. What he did hear, as they hurried past the front desk, was the tall, statuesque woman say that she was checking out of her room. 1312.

Catching hold of Natalie's arm, he pulled her back.

"What do you think you're—?" she demanded.

He merely pointed toward the front desk. "That's room 1312," he told her.

The woman who was Luke Montgomery's alibi looked vaguely familiar to Natalie. She made the connection when introductions were made. Her name was Erikka Hanson, and she was a model of some moderate fame, on her way back East for a swimsuit shoot.

A genuine redhead, Erikka was a full head taller than Natalie with a complexion that filled dermatologists with envy. Candace, Natalie judged, would have scratched her eyes out, had it come down to a tug of war for Montgomery. Her sister passionately resented any woman who was prettier than she was, and this model was in a class all by herself.

As she introduced herself, Natalie had her ID out to confirm her identity.

"I'm sorry to bother you Ms. Hanson, but I'm investigating a homicide. I need to ask you a couple of questions." She slipped her wallet back into her pocket. The model, she noticed, was busy checking out Matt.

Not exactly a one-man woman, are you? she mused.

"What kind of questions?" Erikka wanted to know.

"Was Luke Montgomery with you in your room last night after the gala?" Natalie asked bluntly.

If the model found the question invasive, she gave no indication. On the contrary, a wide smile curved her more than generous mouth.

"He most certainly was." Each word vibrated with enthusiasm. Montgomery, Natalie concluded, had to be good in bed. No wonder Candace had been put out when the casino mogul didn't want to rekindle their affair.

"What time was he there?" Natalie asked. She had deliberately refrained from mentioning which hours needed verifying.

"The *whole* time," Erikka answered with a heartfelt sigh.

The woman was obviously not a Rhodes scholar, Natalie thought dryly.

"Specifically?" she pressed. Then, in case this word, too, was beyond the model's grasp, she broke it down for the woman. "If you could remember what time he came into your room and what time he left, that would be very helpful."

Erikka paused to sign the credit slip the desk clerk submitted to her. Handing it back, she placed the pen on the counter and thought a moment.

"From the time the gala ended—whenever that was—until this morning." Her smile deepened. "If you think he did something wrong, he didn't." She sighed, clearly reliving a moment or two. "As a matter of fact, he did everything just right."

More than I wanted to know, Natalie thought, suddenly feeling like a voyeur. "Is there somewhere I can reach you in case I have more questions?"

The model looked somewhat impatient, but she foraged through her purse and came up with a card. "That's my agent's number," she pointed to it on the card. "He can usually find me."

Or cover for you. But Natalie forced a smile to her lips as she pocketed the card.

"Thank you for your time," she murmured, then moved away from the reservation desk. Erikka and her considerable luggage went in the opposite direction.

Matt found he had to lengthen his stride to keep up with Natalie. She always moved fast when she was agitated, he recalled. "You don't look very happy," he observed.

Natalie shot him a dirty look. "Why should I be happy? I've spent all day questioning people, and all I have is a dead end."

He'd gotten good at spinning information when it was necessary. "You could think of it as having ruled out several possibilities."

She stopped walking for a moment and gazed at him. He was looking at this in a far more positive light than she was.

"Since when did you become an optimist?"

Optimist was a lot better label than spin doctor, he mused. "Sometimes, in this line of business, you have to be."

They were in the lobby of the casino with its ever-present noise and crowds of people. This was where they should just come to a parting of ways. He knew that the right thing to do would be to let her go back to her home or the precinct or wherever it was she was going. But the frustrated disappointment in her eyes got to him.

He was never going to be over her, Matt thought, no matter what he told himself.

"Have you had lunch yet?" he asked.

An odd little smile came and went from her lips. "I haven't actually had breakfast yet." She'd heard the call about her sister's homicide come in just after hitting a fast-food restaurant. Three bites were all she'd had before her stomach rebelled. She'd thrown the rest away.

"We need to remedy that," Matt told her. "Come with me."

She began to follow, then stopped. Old habits died hard, but he had no right to take charge like that. "Why would I want to do that?" she challenged.

He took a couple of steps to cross back to her. "Because you've been working hard, and you haven't had anything to eat. You need to keep your strength up if you're going to play the part of a bulldog," he said matter-of-factly, then smiled. "Besides, The Janus just landed a first-class world-famous chef, and I'm told he makes a filet mignon that has you believing you've died and gone to heaven."

"I'm not interested in 'dying and going to heaven.' Or eating," she informed him. "What I'm interested in is—"

He finished the sentence for her. "Solving your sister's murder, yes I know. But you can't continue functioning indefinitely on an empty stomach," he insisted. Then he added, "Humor me."

It was the wrong thing to say. She didn't want to

humor him, she wanted to double up her fists and beat on him. She wanted this damn ache in her chest that came up each time she looked at him to go away. She wanted to have never laid eyes on him in the first place. Humoring him didn't even make the top one hundred on her list. "Why would I want to do that?"

"Because," he told her patiently, "if we're going to be working together, there's going to have to be some kind of give and take."

"There already was." The words spilled out, refusing to be dammed up any longer. "As I recall, I gave, you took—and then you threw it back at me."

Was that how she remembered it? "That wasn't the way it played out."

Her expression darkened, making him think of a thunderstorm over the desert. "Oh, wasn't it?"

He didn't want to go into it. Not here, not now. Not ever, actually. But she was forcing him to revisit his actions. "I did what I did for a reason, Natalie."

"Right. I believe the term is 'cold feet.' All the way up to the neck," she said sarcastically. "You suddenly realized that you were making a commitment, and it scared the hell out of you."

And why did it still hurt so much, all these years later? *Why aren't I over you, damn it?*

Someone jostled him. Matt hardly noticed. His entire attention was focused on the petite spitfire before him. The woman, if the gods had been kinder, who would have been his wife for several years now. Maybe even the mother of his children. "Is that what you think?"

"Yes," Natalie bit off. "That is *exactly* what I think."

He tried to take hold of her arms, but she shrugged him off. "You're wrong."

"Then what was your reason?" she challenged. "Why would you leave me that way without so much as a decent explanation?"

The answer was very simple. "Because if I gave you one, you would have tried to talk me out of it." He knew how she thought. In her place, he would have done the same thing. But he hadn't been in her place; he'd been in his and the action he took was necessary. "And what I did was for the best."

"Right. For the best," she mocked. "Whose best? Yours?"

"No." *Damn it, you little idiot, I did it because I loved you.* "Yours."

Lifting her chin, she tossed her head defiantly. Her short brown hair swayed from the movement. "I don't believe you. You're only saying that because you think it makes you out to be noble. Well, you're not. You're a coward," she spat out.

He took a firm hold of her shoulders. This time he didn't let her shrug him off. People were watching, and he didn't want this getting back to anyone.

"There's no point in arguing about it, Natalie. It's all in the past."

No, she thought. *Not all of it.* She only wished from the bottom of her heart that it was. But her feelings were very much alive and in the present. But that was her problem, not his.

"You're right," she replied in a monotone voice. "It is."

Touching her, even so slightly, had awakened so many feelings he was incapable of burying. He found himself not wanting her to leave. "About that lunch," he prodded.

Natalie stared at him. "How can you possibly think I'd want to break bread with you after—after—" Frustrated, she couldn't even find the words to finish her sentence.

"Because you need to keep up your strength," he repeated, "and you're going to have to eat sometime. Might as well be something good and on the house. C'mon." He nodded toward his right. "The restaurant is this way." Then, in case she was going to take offense at his leading again, he added, "I know you don't exactly know your way around The Janus."

There was no denying that. Still, she thought of turning on her heel and just walking away. Of letting Matt lead the way only to turn around at the restaurant to find that she had gone.

But in the end, she followed him.

This was business, strictly business, she told herself, and to act on her impulse would have been petulant. She did need Matt as long as her investigation took her into the heart of Montgomery's casino, and she had a feeling that somehow, some way, Candace's death was tied to her coming here last night.

The restaurant was only doing a moderate amount of business. It was the lull between lunch and dinner, and the pace was less hectic. The waitress came to take their order barely minutes after the hostess had shown them to a table.

Matt ordered the meal he'd mentioned earlier, then looked at Natalie who was perusing the oversized, velvet-covered menu. He didn't want to rush her. "Need more time?"

"No, let's get this over with." It was a cruel thing to say, but she felt herself sinking fast. Agreeing to eat with him had been a mistake. She could feel it in her bones. Natalie surrendered her menu to the waitress. "I'll have what he's having," she told the young woman.

"This isn't penance, you know," he told her, focusing on her first statement.

She looked at him pointedly. "Isn't it?" And then she raised her hand, as if to erase her words from an invisible chalkboard. "Sorry. I should be more professional than that. I usually *am* more professional than that. It's just that I never expected to see you again," she confessed. "And it's kind of thrown me."

That smile she'd always loved curved one half of his mouth. Unsettling her stomach. "Welcome to my world."

She shook her head. Ignoring him and the effect he had on her was getting to be impossible. But she was determined to go down fighting. "I'll pass, thanks," she said.

Several minutes passed. Despite the low level din around them, silence sat like an awkward, uninvited guest at their table, making them both feel uncomfortable.

It had never been like this, Matt thought. Not even from the very start. He took a stab at stereotypical conversation. "So what have you been doing with yourself, besides becoming a police detective?"

"That's about it," she said, her tone sealing the doorway that led into her life. "You? Where did life take you after you made your escape?"

"I didn't escape, Natalie," he pointed out patiently. "I did it for your own good."

Second verse, same as the first, she thought. "You

broke my heart for my own good," she mocked. "How do you figure that?"

There was no point in rehashing this. He couldn't go into specifics. "I don't want to get into it now."

"Of course not. Because you're making it up as you go along, and you're at a loss where to go next with this. News flash, I'm not buying. Any of it." Suddenly making up her mind, she stood up. "You know what? I'm not hungry."

He glanced to the side and saw the waitress approaching with their meals. "Why don't you stay a while?" he coaxed. "The waitress is coming with the food."

"You eat it. Or don't. Take it home in a doggie bag, or leave it here. I really don't care," she informed him. And with that, she stormed away.

All she wanted was to get out of the restaurant and the casino. And most of all, she wanted to get away from him.

Chapter 8

Natalie got as far as the other side of the Rainbow Room's entrance.

That was where Matt, after tossing down several bills on their table to cover the meal they weren't having, managed to catch up to her. Taking hold of her shoulders, he swung Natalie around to face him. Agitated, trying to deal with a host of jumbled emotions, he hadn't the faintest idea what he was going to say to her.

As it turned out, he didn't say anything.

Instead, he acted. Before he knew it, his instincts had taken over and completely overruled even a glimmer of common sense.

Matt brought his mouth down on hers before he could think better of it or try to stop himself.

He didn't want to stop himself.

Natalie struggled to pull back for less than half a

heartbeat. That's all the time it took for her longing and the hunger that was eating away at her to kick in. It surged through her veins like a runaway wildfire.

A bittersweet feeling of homecoming washed over her. Her mind, all but spinning out of control, just utterly shut down.

She was instantly propelled eight years into the past as a tidal wave of euphoria materialized out of nowhere, sweeping over her. Robbing her of her senses as she clung to him.

God she'd missed him. Missed the feeling that only he could create inside her.

Not that she let anyone else even try. She hadn't taken any relationship on a test drive since theirs had ended. Hadn't even allowed herself to become involved in one. It was far too much trouble. She'd become all work, no play. Relationships brought the specter of heartache with them, and her quota had been filled up for a lifetime.

Besides, Candace went out with enough men for both of them. There was no need for her to participate in this madness. So, for the last eight years, she'd been a virtual nun.

She wasn't acting like a nun now.

Deep down in her bones, Natalie knew she shouldn't be doing this, knew that this momentary aberration had just made her life a hundred percent harder. The amount of backpedaling that was going to be required to balance this out was going to be enormous.

But for this tiny island of time, it didn't matter to her.

All that mattered was riding this lightning bolt until it disintegrated beneath her feet.

Her arms tightened around his neck as her body sealed itself to his.

How had he managed to survive without this? Without her in his life? How had he managed to wake up each morning without finding her in his bed? Right at this moment, he hadn't a clue.

All his noble reasons for walking away from her turned to confetti and blew away in the wind like so many tiny squares of colored paper.

The feel of her body against his lit a fire in his veins. If they weren't out in the open like this, in a public place undoubtedly garnering attention, he would have swept Natalie up in his arms and taken her to his bed— or to any handy flat surface in a pinch. And succumbing to a moment of weakness, undo everything that had cost him so much to do in the first place. Leaving her hadn't even been the hardest part. Staying away was.

He still loved her.

If he'd harbored any doubts about that, they were gone now. Moreover, he was *still* in love with her, which was a completely different thing, and even he could understand the basic distinction now.

Lost in a fog, Matt was thinking more clearly than he had these last agonizing eight years. Passion filled him as he deepened the kiss.

Struggling to find the strength that she'd always prided herself on possessing, Natalie finally managed to wedge her hands against his chest and push Matt back.

"I had no idea you'd be that grateful for a doggie bag," she quipped hoarsely. Clearing her throat, she searched for her bearings as well as her voice. "I have to get going."

"Natalie—" he began, not really certain what it was that he wanted to say, only that he didn't want her to leave. Not yet. Not after he'd discovered that the passion between them was just as red-hot as ever. Maybe even more so.

She looked into his eyes and could see what he was thinking. Maybe because the same thoughts had raced across her mind.

"This doesn't change anything," she told him. "You still left me. Still hurt me. One kiss, no matter how hot, isn't going to erase that or mend any of the fences that you broke in your hurry to leave."

Reluctantly, Matt withdrew his hands from her waist. "I know."

But you could try, damn it. You could pretend to go through the motions. Tell me you were stupid and wrong. I'll listen.

Disappointment filled all the crevices that passion had just occupied. Matt had given up much too easily. Pulling herself together, Natalie glanced at her watch. She really did have to go. Her father had said something about wanting her present at the emergency family meeting he was calling. He'd mentioned four o'clock. Even if she drove with her siren on, she was going to be late.

But then, probably so were the others. No one in the Rothchild family was known for punctuality. She was the one who came the closest. Her stepsister, Silver, didn't even own a watch. But then, Silver was a rock star who moved to her own inner timepiece.

"I've got to go," she repeated, doing her best to sound cool and removed, even though her body temperature was still bordering on feverish, thanks to him. "Call me if you find out anything new that has to do with Candace," she instructed.

"Can I call you if I don't?" He hadn't meant to say that, but then, he hadn't meant to kiss her, either. An afternoon in her presence and all his control seemed to splinter into useless pieces.

"No."

The single word hung in the air as she turned on her heel and quickly walked away. Before she broke down and sealed her mouth to his again. He was an addiction. She'd only fooled herself into thinking she'd kicked it. It owned her.

To her surprise, half a beat later, Matt fell into place beside her. Annoyed, Natalie stopped walking. "Where do you think you're going?"

"With you," he replied simply. "You said you wanted me to work with you, remember?"

"I was referring to here, at The Janus." God knew she knew better than to have him around for any length of time beyond that. If she'd thought otherwise, her reaction to his kiss showed her just how weak she was when it came to him.

Matt shrugged in response to her answer. "Two heads are better than one."

A sarcastic remark hovered on her tongue, but never made it to her lips. In this case, the direct approach was better. "Not this time. I'm due at the house. My father is calling an emergency family meeting. Last I looked, you weren't family." *And whose fault is that?* she added silently.

"No," he agreed, "but maybe you could use the moral support."

She took it as a direct slam about her inner strength. Her eyes narrowed as she informed him, "I can handle my father."

His tone was nonconfrontational. He wasn't trying to get into a fight; he just wanted to help. When they'd been together, she was the one who'd wanted the kind of family that could only be found in human interest stories and carefully crafted feel-good movies.

"Never said you couldn't. But I hear that your new stepmother is a piece of work."

It was more than true but would have required some interaction on his part to learn for himself. "How long did you say you were back?"

"A couple of weeks." He guessed the reason behind her question. "Word gets around fast," Matt told her. *Especially when you ask questions*, he added silently.

"Thanks, but showing up with you would be like waving a red flag in my father's face. He doesn't really like you," she told him honestly.

Matt laughed shortly. "Yeah, I know. He made that pretty clear."

Her curiosity was instantly aroused. Just how full had those two weeks of his been? Had he come around the mansion without her knowing it?

"When?"

It was ancient history. Matt saw no reason to keep it secret any longer. "When he tried to buy me off."

That didn't make any sense. How could her father try to buy him off—and why would he?—if he had a cash flow problem? "I thought that your family supposedly lent my father money so he could get out of the financial hole he was in."

"That's now. I'm talking about before."

Natalie still wasn't following him. "How much before?"

He waved her question away. Maybe he shouldn't have said anything. "Doesn't matter."

"It does to me," she insisted. Her eyes pinned him in place. He wasn't going anywhere and neither was she until he answered her question. "*When* did my father offer you money?"

"Before." The expression on her face indicated that the single word did nothing to satisfy her curiosity, so he gave her more. "Eight years ago."

She felt her heart twist. She'd been better off not knowing. "That's why you left? Because he paid you off?" she asked incredulously. "Why you son of a bit—" Stunned, speechless, she raised her hand, ready to slap him across the face at the insult.

Matt caught her wrist, blocking contact. He knew that for simplicity's sake, he should hold his peace and let her believe the worst about him. But something wouldn't let him. He didn't want her believing that he had been bought off.

She could think he was a rotten human being, not worth her time and certainly not her love, but he didn't want her believing that she'd been cast aside for thirty pieces of silver.

"He *tried* to buy me off," he corrected. "Offered me a bit of money, actually. Back then, your father thought you were worth a quarter of a million dollars. Or maybe that was what getting rid of me was worth to him, I don't know. *But I didn't take it,*" he told her, emphasizing each word.

Confusion washed over her. "If you didn't leave because of the money—" A wave of jealousy struck. "Was there someone else?"

His eyes met hers. "You know better than that, Natalie."

"No, I don't." She sighed, weary of this uncertain feeling she'd been carrying around with her. It wouldn't matter if she didn't feel anything for him, but she did. She wanted answers. "I don't know better than that. *Why* did you leave me?"

There was nothing to be gained by this. "It's in the past, Natalie. Let it go."

If only she could. She'd tried hard enough, Lord knows, but she'd never gotten to that point. "I can't."

"Yes you can," he assured her firmly. This was an argument that was not about to be resolved. Not now, not ever. "If you don't want me coming with you, I won't," he agreed. "But you're going to be late if you don't get going."

He was giving her the bum's rush. Okay for now, she conceded reluctantly. But the gateway to the past had opened, if just a crack. She intended to wedge a crowbar into the tiny space and work it until she managed to open it up all the way.

But right now, she wasn't up to waging potentially futile battles, so she turned away without a word and just kept walking. Wishing with all her heart that she had never set eyes on Matt Schaffer. Or that, at the very least, he was still back in Los Angeles.

She didn't need this type of anguish on top of Candace's murder.

Candace.

She was her top priority. All that mattered was

finding out who killed her sister. Finding it out and bringing the bastard down. Whatever that took.

The wide, winding driveway before the mansion that she had once called home was packed with various expensive automobiles. Hers looked like a poor relation. Poor, but energy conscious, she thought wryly.

Recognizing the other vehicles, she realized that she was probably the last to arrive. Couldn't be helped, Natalie thought.

Couldn't it? a small, inner voice mocked. *You didn't need to kiss him back. Didn't need to stand there, talking to him, hanging on his every word the way you used to.*

Wow, now she was getting into an argument with herself. She was *really* losing it, Natalie thought.

Might as well go in and get this over with, she told herself.

When she rang the doorbell, Clive opened the door almost immediately. His expression appeared to be rigid until he saw it was her. And then he smiled, as if to say, "Ah, the normal one."

Natalie was about to ask the butler if he had stationed himself at the front door to get as far away from her family as possible when she was interrupted by a crash that sounded as if it was coming from the living room.

She raised her eyes quizzically up to Clive's face.

"That would be Master Ricky," he informed her, answering her unspoken question.

She frowned. Her half brother was a whirling dervish in search of an accident. A walking example of Attention Deficit Disorder, he constantly left chaos in his wake. Her father was at a loss how to handle him and his mother, Rebecca Lynn, refused to, believing the boy was better off if he was allowed to "express" himself.

This did not have the makings of a good outcome. "Dad called a family meeting, but I thought he meant adults only."

"Sadly, no," Clive told her. "Miss Rebecca Lynn wants Master Ricky present. She said something about Miss Candace being an object lesson for him."

On how not to live your life, apparently, Natalie thought. She couldn't help taking umbrage for Candace even though she felt that *no one* should attempt to emulate her late twin's lifestyle. But then everything connected with her stepmother seemed to irritate her to no end. The woman was like a rash for which there was no cure.

And her father seemed apparently blind to all of his wife's shortcomings.

Reluctant to walk into the lion's den, Natalie stalled for a moment. "How's the meeting coming along?" she asked the butler.

A whimsical half smile fleetingly played along the older man's lips. "No one has killed anyone yet."

"Always a good sign," Natalie agreed.

She unconsciously squared her shoulders, the way she always did when she was about to face Stepmother 2.0—which was the way she'd taken to referring to Rebecca Lynn. The thinly veiled animosity between the woman and the rest of the family had never really died down.

Too bad her father'd had that midlife crisis of his. Instead of buying a new sports car—he already had more than ten housed within his cavernous garage—he'd shed his second wife and married a woman young enough to be his daughter.

As far as she was concerned, Natalie had always pre-ferred her father's last wife. Anne Worth Rothchild not only had pedigree but she had class. She was a lady in every sense of the word. In contrast, Rebecca Lynn was a grasping gold digger in every sense of *that* word.

Try as she might, she just couldn't get herself to like Rebecca Lynn, or her spoiled brat of a half brother. The only male heir in the family, Ricky, even at this tender age, radiated an aura of entitlement. Something, Natalie had no doubt, that had been taught to him by his mother. As someone who preferred to earn her own way, she found it absolutely repugnant.

Rebecca Lynn, Natalie was certain, was angling to be become the sole heir of the Rothchild fortune—once Harold Rothchild passed on.

Over her dead body, Natalie vowed. Not that she wanted *any* of the money. She just didn't want Rebecca Lynn getting her hands on it exclusively.

Natalie stopped just short of the living room. As a matter of fact, now that she thought about it, Candace's sudden death dovetailed nicely with their stepmother's plans. She'd bet her last dime that Rebecca Lynn would have liked nothing better than to have Candace's fate befall her and her two remaining siblings—her sister Jenna and stepsister Silver.

Can't tell the players apart without a scorecard, Natalie thought dryly.

Forcing herself to walk into the living room, Natalie saw her youngest sibling, Jenna, a self-assured twenty-five-year-old, currently heading up her own party planning business, crouching on the floor. She was busy picking up the pieces of what had been, until moments ago, a colorful vase from a trip to Hawaii.

The vase, for reasons unknown, had suffered Ricky's sudden displeasure. He would have gone on a rampage except that Harold had grabbed him.

Rebecca Lynn took immediate possession of their son, giving her husband a dark, censoring look. When that faded, it was replaced by a disdainful expression that took up residence on her perfectly made-up face.

Everything about the woman screamed "fake," Natalie couldn't help thinking. Rebecca Lynn's hair was currently a riotous cloud of red that could not be found anywhere in nature.

Silver, Anna's daughter, was sitting over in a corner, her expression barring anyone from attempting to approach her.

Ever the outsider. Although, from what she'd heard, in the last few years, Silver and Candace had actually gotten closer. However, the relationship had come about for all the wrong reasons, at least when it came to Candace, who had orchestrated the "friendship." Her twin had been extremely jealous of their stepsister. Silver, who was the same age as they were, had been born beautiful. With her mother's support, she had become a singing sensation by the time she turned sixteen. This after bringing the modeling world to its knees.

Silver, Natalie had always felt, could have become anything she wanted to be.

Looking around the room at the various members of her extended—or was that distended?—family, Natalie viewed them all with a disparaging eye and now just shook her head.

Talk about dysfunctional families. Hers would probably be up for some kind of prize—if there were prizes given for something like this.

His temper on edge because Rebecca Lynn had usurped his authority to discipline their son—again— Harold Rothchild looked at the latecomer with no attempt to hide his displeasure.

"So you've finally decided to grace us with your presence."

"Yup, finally," Natalie echoed in the same tone her father had just used.

So far, it'd been one hell of a day, and the rest of it wasn't shaping up to be any better. Making her way over to a chair that was near Silver, Natalie sat down. Her stepsister slanted a glance in her direction and nodded a silent greeting.

"All right," Natalie said, bracing herself for anything. "Let's get on with it."

Chapter 9

After Natalie took her seat, Harold didn't begin speaking immediately. Instead, he moved restlessly about the wide, cathedral-ceilinged living room like a caged man desperately searching for the way out and only coming up against dead ends.

Finally, his back to the baby grand piano his wife insisted on getting for their son, he said, "By now, you've all heard the news. Candace is dead."

"Is that why you called us here, to make sure we all knew?" Silver asked incredulously, raising her voice to be heard over her stepbrother's high-pitched whining. "There's been nothing else all over the news all morning," she pointed out.

"No, I called you together because we need to make funeral arrangements." His intense blue eyes shifted toward his wife.

Rebecca Lynn took immediate offense. "Hey, don't look at me. I've never handled things like that." A disdainful expression crossed her face. "Funerals give me the creeps."

Anything that required work gave the woman the creeps, Natalie thought. "Eloquently put," she murmured under her breath.

The general tone, since the words were not audible, earned her a dirty look from her stepmother. Bored and frustrated, Ricky's whining went up a notch. It was a little like walking into an insane asylum, Natalie realized.

Her father shifted his attention to her. "Natalie, exactly when can we expect to have your sister's body released?"

Her father was a reasonably intelligent man. He should have known the answer to that. And then it occurred to her that he expected her to have some kind of special pull at the coroner's office. The system didn't work like that.

"As soon as the ME finishes the autopsy and determines the cause of death," she replied patiently.

Horror registered on Silver's face. "You mean they're gutting her like some kind of fish?" she asked, not bothering to stifle a shiver.

"We know the cause of death," Jenna insisted. When Natalie looked at her, waiting, her younger sister declared, "Someone killed her."

Was everyone being deliberately obtuse, or had the fuse on her temper been shortened by Matt's sudden reappearance into her life?

"That's not the cause, that's the effect," Natalie explained, trying to at least sound patient. "If we know how, we might know who."

"What good is that going to do us?" Jenna asked sullenly. "She'll still be dead."

"No, Natalie's right," Harold cut in. "If we know who, then we'll know if killing Candace was personal—or personal." Was his daughter killed by a jealous lover, or someone who had it in for the family, for him, and this was their way of striking out?

A loud, exasperated sound escaped from Rebecca Lynn's lips. The other women in the room all looked in her direction. "Okay, you've officially gone off the deep end," she told her husband nastily.

"Don't go declaring him mentally incompetent just yet, Rebecca Lynn, although I'm sure that the thought is near and dear to your heart," Natalie said, a deliberately fake smile on her lips. Turning to her father, her "smile" vanished. "Just what do you mean by that?" she wanted to know.

Before Harold could say anything, Rebecca Lynn presented herself to him, her hands fisted at her waist. "Are you going to let her talk to me like that?" she demanded.

"Why not?" Silver interjected. "You talk to him like that all the time."

Whatever heated words Rebecca Lynn retorted to her stepdaughter were drowned out by Ricky's screams because no one was paying any attention to him. The next moment, he was scrambling up onto the piano bench and banging on the keys, adding yet another layer of dissonance to the cacophony.

Jenna's voice was almost shrill as she demanded, "Will someone *please* shut that kid up?"

Harold looked as if he was down to his very last

nerve as he implored his wife, "Rebecca, please, take him out of here."

Rebecca Lynn crossed her arms before her, a portrait of immovable stubbornness. Everyone in the room knew that there was nothing she hated more than to appear as if she was being ordered around. "Why don't you? He's your son, too."

Though she wanted nothing more than to just withdraw and go home, Natalie found herself coming to her father's rescue.

"In case you hadn't noticed, Dad's the one who called the meeting." Rebecca Lynn patently ignored her and picked up her all but empty second glass of gin and tonic. She'd raised it to her lips when Natalie added, "But I'll be happy to take my little brother out of here."

A look of alarm descended over Rebecca Lynn's face. Swallowing a curse, she set her glass down hard on the coffee table and quickly rose to her feet. Striding across the room, she grabbed her son by the hand and yanked him off the piano bench. The boy's screams only swelled in volume. Glaring at Natalie, Rebecca Lynn dragged her son from the room.

Ricky was heard kicking and screaming all the way up the stairs to his room.

If she knew Rebecca Lynn, Ricky was quickly going to become the housekeeper's problem, Natalie thought, feeling sorry for the older woman.

Harold took advantage of Rebecca Lynn's absence. His young wife had a way of intimidating him that neither Anna, nor June—the late, lamented love of his life—ever had. "Can't you put some pressure on this ME of yours?" he asked Natalie. "I want to get Candace buried and put this whole nasty business behind us as soon as possible."

"He's not my ME," Natalie pointed out, then realized something. "You're worried that this is just the beginning, aren't you?"

"What do you mean, just the beginning?" Confused, Jenna looked from her father to her sister. "Just the beginning of what?"

"Nothing," Harold dismissed Jenna's question much too quickly. The look he shot Natalie said that he'd told her what he had in confidence.

If she'd felt that this only involved Rebecca Lynn, she wouldn't have said a word in front of Silver and Jenna. But her father had given her the impression that this thing went beyond her grasping stepmother and her unruly half brother.

Natalie looked pointedly at her father, passionately wishing he had a backbone. "They have a right to know, Dad."

Jenna's eyes nervously shifted from her to their father. "Know what?"

Since her father still wasn't saying anything, Natalie took the matter into her own hands. "Dad thinks that the ring is cursed."

It still didn't make any sense. Jenna exchanged looks with Silver, who looked no more enlightened than she felt. "What ring?" Jenna wanted to know.

Again, Natalie waited for her father to say something. He didn't. So she did. "The Tears of the Quetzal."

The mention of the priceless diamond dissipated the fog Silver seemed to be encased in. They all knew that the gem was rumored to be theirs. Half the time, she thought it was all a myth, made up by her stepfather to court publicity.

"What does that have to do with Candace's—?" Silver stopped abruptly as the realization suddenly occurred to her. "Was Candace wearing the ring when she was killed last night?"

"Either the ring, or a damn good paste imitation," Natalie answered. But they all knew Candace. Her late twin couldn't abide fakes. She took great satisfaction in flaunting the real thing. The stone had certainly looked real enough on the casino tapes she'd viewed. "When they interviewed her on camera last night, just before she walked into The Janus, Candace was waving her hand around for all the world to see."

"Then anyone could have broken into her condo and killed her for it," Jenna speculated.

"Yes," Natalie agreed. "Except for one thing." The two women and her father looked at her, waiting. "Candace knew her killer."

"What makes you say that?" Jenna demanded, sounding almost hostile about the suggestion.

"There was no sign of forced entry," Natalie told them. "The room where they found her was a mess, as if she was trying to fight off whoever she'd chosen to bring home with her. But it was obvious that she was the one who had opened the door in the first place."

Harold sighed and sat down in the winged armchair that his wife had vacated. He closed his eyes wearily. "I always knew this was going to happen."

The nature of Natalie's job forced her to look beyond the obvious and delve deeper. She gave her father's words a different interpretation. He wasn't talking about her twin's lifestyle.

"You're talking about the curse, aren't you?" Harold seemed almost beaten down, and he made no answer. He merely lifted his shoulders in a half shrug before letting them fall again. The ring was part of family lore, but to her recollection, her father had never elaborated on it. "Just why is this ring supposed to be cursed?"

"There's no such thing as curses," Jenna snapped. She ran her hands up and down her arms even though the day had been unseasonably warm. "I wish you'd all just stop talking about it."

"It doesn't matter why," Harold told Natalie, his voice weary but firm. As far as he was concerned, the subject was closed. "It just is, Natalie. Let's leave it at that."

But she had no intention of tiptoeing around the subject because it seemed to upset her father and, for different reasons, Jenna. She didn't like unanswered questions.

Natalie tried to make him understand. "Sure it matters. Say, if it was originally stolen from someone, then we're looking at a revenge motive. If this is nothing more than some kind of 'curse' handed down through the ages, then we're looking for some kind of wraith or ghoul, and we're going to need to get ourselves a ghost buster."

It took Harold a moment to realize that she wasn't serious about the second half of her reasoning. He scowled at her. "This isn't funny, Natalie."

"No," she agreed. "Death never is." She studied his face. "Now, is there something more you want to tell us about this ring, Dad?"

There was no hesitation on his part as he barked, "No."

There was something else going on here, she could swear to it.

"Then why do you look like you've got something to hide?" she asked, trying her best to keep her voice neutral.

"Stop badgering my husband," Rebecca Lynn ordered as she walked back into the room. Ricky, mercifully, was nowhere in sight.

Natalie really hated the woman's high-handed manner. "He was our father before he was your husband, Rebecca Lynn," she informed her stepmother. Glancing at her father, she felt sorry for him. He suddenly looked a great deal older than his sixty years. "But, for now, I'll back off."

Harold attempted to flash a smile of thanks toward her, but the corners of his mouth hardly rose.

"We still haven't talked about Candace's funeral arrangements," he pointed out heavily, uttering each word as if it weighed a ton.

"Oh God," Rebecca Lynn moaned, rolling her brown eyes heavenward. "Just put her into the ground and be done with it."

Natalie instantly took offense for her late twin. Granted Candace had a myriad of faults, but she was dead and deserved respect. She threw up her hands in exasperation. "I'll take care of it, Dad," she told him.

Harold looked as if a huge boulder had been lifted off his shoulders. "You really will?"

"Yes, I really will." What choice did she have? She could see this "family meeting" degenerating into name-calling and buck passing. She didn't need to be part of that. "As soon as her body is released, I'll have Candace cremated and place her urn in the family crypt—beside Grandpa."

Silver suddenly spoke up. "What about a service?" she wanted to know.

That was easy enough to address. "We'll have a memorial service," Natalie told her. "Just for the family."

But even that drew an objection from Rebecca Lynn. Hostility entered her voice. "You're not planning to include that woman, are you?"

They all knew that "that woman" was Rebecca Lynn's way of referring to Anna Worth Rothchild, the ex-wife Harold had unceremoniously dumped in order to wed his current trophy wife.

"I most certainly am," Natalie informed her. She would have invited her former stepmother even if it hadn't irritated her present one. That it did was just icing on the cake. "Anna was like a mother to Candace."

Fuming, Rebecca Lynn spun around on her heel and looked at her husband, expecting him to back up her position. "Harold!"

She was unpleasantly surprised. "She's right," Harold replied. He looked like a mongoose that had accidentally fallen into a snake pit.

Rebecca Lynn refused to accept defeat. "But she wasn't her mother, was she?"

Her stepmother's high-handed tone finally managed to arouse Silver's ire. "If my mother wants to come, she can come," the child-star-turned-pop-diva spat out.

Rebecca Lynn glared at her stepdaughter, barely refraining from a bevy of ripe words. She knew she was outnumbered, but refused to admit she was outmaneuvered. Turning to Harold, she delivered her ultimatum with a dramatic toss of her head. Flaming red hair undulated all around her.

"If that woman comes to the service, Harold, then I won't."

"And miss a chance to be photographed by the paparazzi?" Natalie asked, feigned surprise. The look on her face told her stepmother that she was as transparent as a glass of water. "I sincerely doubt that, but the choice," she said pleasantly, "is yours."

Furious, Rebecca Lynn stormed out of the room, cursing them all to several levels of hell, each hotter than the last.

Harold merely shook his head. Though he was still under her thumb, his new wife had lost much of her charm for him. "You really shouldn't antagonize her like that, Natalie."

In response, Natalie smiled at him. "Rebecca Lynn makes it much too easy, and I have such few simple pleasures."

Harold didn't bother commenting. Instead, he asked, "How's the investigation going?"

As she started to answer, Natalie noticed Jenna edging closer, as if afraid she might miss something. That was a surprise, she thought. She would have expected that from Silver, who, thanks to Candace's deceptive machinations, thought of Candace as her friend.

With five years between them, Jenna and Candace had never known a close moment—again, thanks mainly to Candace. But then, Natalie reflected, maybe she'd misjudged her younger sister.

It wouldn't have been the first time her judgment had failed her, Natalie reminded herself.

Her father was looking at her expectantly. Did he

think she was some kind of a magician? "It's only been a day, Dad. I'm still following leads."

An impatient sound escaped his lips. "And you'll tell me when you find out who?"

When, not *if.* He either had a lot of faith in her or was playing the guilt card. Most likely the latter, Natalie decided.

A spasmodic smile came and went from her lips. "You'll be the first to know."

"Do you have any, you know, suspects?" Jenna asked.

The immediate male population. Out loud, Natalie said, "Someone the camera caught Candace smiling at."

Jenna's eyes widened. Natalie thought she heard her stop breathing. "Who?"

"Unfortunately, the person was *off* camera, so we don't know. But I'm doing my best to try to piece it all together."

"If anyone can do it, my money's on you, Nat," Jenna said.

Natalie said nothing. She only wished she had half the confidence that Jenna had.

Natalie remained at the mansion another hour or so after her sister's departure. Her father detained her with his incessant questions about the murder investigation, while stressing how crucial it was to locate the mystical ring that was all but a third party in all this. Finally disentangling herself from him, she went home to see if she could make any more headway with the copies of the tapes that Matt had given her.

It took a little doing before she could pull them up on her own computer. The computer, she had long ago decided, was not her friend.

But she did what she could and made progress using baby steps.

Engrossed, Natalie didn't hear the doorbell at first. And then, when the repeated noise finally penetrated her consciousness, she decided to ignore it.

But whoever was ringing the doorbell patently refused to be ignored. It went on pealing, setting her teeth on edge.

With a sigh, Natalie rose from her desk and crossed to the front door.

She paused only long enough to get her service revolver.

In her experience, it was never a given who was on the other side of the door, and she had to admit that her father had looked spooked enough about this curse business to at least make her take a small measure of precaution. And even if she didn't believe in curses, as a police detective she knew that she was a living, breathing target for some wacko looking to even some imaginary score.

"Who is it?" she called out as she approached the door.

"Delivery boy."

Was that—?

No, it couldn't be. It couldn't be Matt. He didn't know where she lived. She'd sold the condo where they'd been together, bought this place and took strict care to remain unlisted and off everyone's radar. This was just her imagination, working overtime.

Reaching the door, she said, "I didn't order anything."

"Look, lady, all I know is that your name's on this bill."

Definitely Matt. She'd know his voice anywhere. But what was he doing here?

Still holding her weapon, its safety off, Natalie opened the door.

The gun was the first thing Matt noticed. "You can put that away," he told her. Opening his jacket with one hand, he held the side out for her inspection. "I'm unarmed."

After a long pause, she finally put up her weapon. But she still held the door ajar and made no move to get out of the way. "What are you doing here, Matt?" she wanted to know.

"Bringing you the dinner you abandoned earlier." He held up the pristine white bag. The Janus's logo was on the side. "Knowing you, I figured you didn't take the time to stop and eat."

Her eyes narrowed. *I'm not the person I used to be. The one whose heart you stomped on.* "You *don't* know me," she informed him tersely.

He looked as if he was willing to give her the benefit of the doubt. "Did you stop to eat?"

She realized she could lie and be done with it, sending him on his way. Why she didn't was beyond her. "No, I didn't."

His mouth curved. "I rest my case. And I'd like to rest this—" he indicated the large bag he was holding "—because it's getting hot."

She frowned, then stepped back, opening the door wider. "I can't help feeling like I've just opened my door to the Trojan horse."

Walking in, Matt grinned at her. Her stomach tightened instantly. "Don't worry, there're no tiny men wearing armor in the bag."

It wasn't tiny men in armor she was worried about. It was the very large, very real one who was walking into her house that concerned her.

Chapter 10

Natalie pointed Matt toward her kitchen.

He crossed to it quickly, setting the bag down on the table. Then he went to the sink and ran cold water over his hands to take the sting out.

"So how did the family meeting go?" he asked in a conversational tone. When she didn't answer, he looked at her over his shoulder. Natalie returned her weapon to its holster, putting the safety back on. "I figured you might want to vent a little."

She handed Matt a dish towel to dry his hands. "Why are you being so nice?" she inquired.

Taking the towel, he dried his hands, then left the towel on the counter. "Why do you always have to question everything? Just accept what's happening."

Natalie folded the towel and put it back in its place.

"I did that once and had my heart ripped out of my chest. I'm a little more cautious these days."

His eyes were drawn to her hands. "You're not married." It was a rhetorical statement. He already knew that.

Her first instinct was to hide her hands behind her back, but she didn't. Instead, she took out a handful of napkins from a supply she kept in the pantry.

"No."

"Were you?" he pressed, watching her move about the kitchen. "Ever?"

She shot him an impatient look. "Did you bring dinner or a questionnaire?" And then she sighed as she took out two tall glasses from the cupboard. "No," she answered stiffly. "I've never been married. I decided that the male species was just too unstable to build a relationship with or to trust."

He had the good grace to wince. "Ouch."

Moving Matt aside, she opened the bag he had brought and saw that there were two large covered containers inside it instead of just one. Natalie raised her eyes to his face.

"There're two portions here."

His expression was the soul of innocence. "I didn't eat, either."

Removing first one container, then the other, she placed them both on the table.

"And they're still warm."

He nodded interceptively. "They do some pretty magical things in that Rainbow kitchen."

"The waitress was bringing these out eight hours ago—when I left," she reminded him. Natalie opened the containers one at a time, and a small cloud of steam emerged from each.

He spread his hands wide, adding a little shrug at the end. "Like I said, magical."

Yeah, right. "You ordered fresh portions, didn't you?"

Why was he going through all this trouble for someone he'd walked out on? Someone he made no effort to contact in the last eight years? Why was he messing with her like this?

Matt held his hands up in front of her, his wrists touching as if he expected to be led off in handcuffs. "I always loved that steel-trap mind of yours. Take me away, Officer Rothchild."

She had a very real urge to double up her fist and punch him in the arm.

"That's Detective Rothchild," she corrected, then shook her head and blew out a loud sigh, hoping that it would sufficiently distract him from seeing the involuntary smile on her lips. But Natalie could see by his grin that he hadn't missed it. "Idiot," she pronounced.

There was no arguing with that. "In more ways than one," he assured her.

This time, her sigh was weary. "Why are you talking in riddles?"

The serious lapse was gone. "I thought women liked men of mystery."

Oh no, he wasn't going to suck her into an exchange of banter. She wanted some kind of answers.

"We were way past the 'liking' stage once, Schaffer." Taking out two forks and steak knives, she deposited them on the table, then took down two dinner plates to join them. "You were the one who left, not me."

He watched her move around, taking in every fluid motion. A deep-seated longing took root. "We can still be friends."

"No," she replied emphatically, "we can't. I'm not one of those broad-minded women who thinks that turning her exes into 'pals' is the adult thing to do."

He looked confused. "Then why did you ask me to help you?"

Natalie deposited the contents of one container onto a plate, then followed suit with the other. She flung the empty containers into the lined garbage pail beneath her sink before answering.

"Because, whether I liked it or not, I needed your help. You got me the tapes—thank you," she tagged on as an afterthought, the two words all but burning her tongue as she uttered them.

He knew that cost her, and he couldn't help being amused. "You're welcome."

"And having you there got me an 'audience' with your boss." She needed to rule her father's chief rival out. "I can bluff my way through this, but the fact of the matter is, I'm a pariah as far as investigating my sister's murder goes."

"You *are* too close," he pointed out.

So much for his taking her side in this, she thought bitterly.

"No one else is close enough," she countered. "It's a high-profile case, but let's face it, we're not exactly without dead bodies in this town. This isn't Parker and Davidson's only homicide."

"And it is yours?" Matt questioned. He was well aware of the fact that the LVPD's homicide division was understaffed.

There were open cases on her desk but none that mattered to her as much as this one. Besides, she couldn't work on them off the job.

"I'm on bereavement leave," she reminded him, "so, yes, right now it is." Moving from the table, she crossed to the refrigerator to get a diet cola for herself. "You want a soda? Or something a little stronger?" she added, recalling that he didn't much care for diet drinks and that was all she stocked in the way of soda.

He opted for the latter. "A little stronger."

She waited for him to follow up his choice with something more specific. "What?"

You.

Matt wondered how she'd respond if he'd said that out loud. Probably tell him to go to hell. But he was there already, because seeing Natalie and not having her was much harder on him than he'd ever thought it would be.

"Vodka, if you have it. Or beer," he amended. From where he sat, he could see into the refrigerator. There were a couple of bottles in the door. "Anything, really. I'm easy."

She turned around, holding two bottles of beer in her hands.

"No," she replied. "You're not." Taking a bottle opener out of the drawer, she flipped the cap off one bottle and then the other. Natalie handed him the first one and rather than sit down, she remained standing over him. "What are you doing here, Matt?"

He avoided her eyes. He'd gotten good at lying, but he never could to her. Which was why he'd left a note in his wake rather than stay to talk to her.

"I told you, I wanted to bring you dinner."

Liar. "Is that the only reason you're here?" she pressed. "To make sure I eat?"

This time he did raise his eyes to hers. "That, and because I still like looking at you, Natalie. You are still one of the most beautiful creatures God ever created."

Wow…he sure did know how to press her buttons. How to torture her.

"I can't do this," she told him suddenly. "I can't do this."

He didn't follow her. "Do what?"

"I can't sit here opposite you and pretend I don't feel anything, that I don't still—"

She didn't get to finish.

Pushing his chair back, Matt was on his feet, sinking his hands into her hair, tilting her face up to his. Immobilizing her lips by feverishly pressing his own against them.

The explosion that occurred within her came just as suddenly. The bottle slipped from her fingers, hitting the floor. It didn't break, but sent up an amber wave that managed to christen both her bare legs and the legs of his slacks.

The splash barely registered on the perimeter of her mind. She was otherwise occupied.

The heat that flared between them swiftly mushroomed in depth and intensity.

Eight years.

Eight years she'd gone without making love. Without feeling like a woman. Everything within her rallied forward to rekindle that old, familiar feeling of sheer ecstasy.

Logically, Natalie knew she should be pushing him away. Knew she should be calling him names and accusing him of all sorts of things, of using her vul-

nerability to satisfy some inner selfish need of his to see
that she still wanted him. Right now, he had all the proof
he could want—and didn't that go a long way toward
feeding his ego?

But even so, she couldn't make herself stop, couldn't
pull back. Couldn't even get her hands to stop their
frantic movements as she yanked away at his clothing,
stripping him of his shirt, his slacks, his underwear,
anything and everything that could get in the way of
what she so desperately needed.

And she was thrilled to feel his hands on her, doing
the exact same thing. Making her clothes vanish and her
body sizzle.

Within seconds, Matt had her on the kitchen floor, his
hands and mouth making love to every inch of her with
the enthusiasm and zeal of a dying man in the desert who
had stumbled onto an oasis filled with water and fig trees.

His mouth was everywhere, setting her skin on fire.

Natalie moaned and twisted beneath his lips,
eagerly scrambling toward the light, toward that
supreme burst of incredible sensation that she hadn't
experienced for so long.

For forever.

It was weak of her and she knew it, but she didn't
care. All she wanted in this moment in time was to stop
feeling like a member of the living dead. And only Matt
could do that for her. Could make her feel, however
briefly, alive again. He was the only man she had ever
wanted. The only man she had ever loved.

How had he managed? Noble intentions or not, how
had he been able to stay away from her for so long
when she was life itself to him? Not to mention that

kissing Natalie's lips was the single biggest turn-on he'd ever experienced.

The more he kissed her, the more he wanted her.

He'd known it would come to this. The second he had agreed to return to Vegas to oversee the overhauling of the security system at The Janus, he'd known that somehow, some way, he would end up here, making passionate love with Natalie.

And feeling whole again.

He hadn't fully realized the extent of just how diminished he'd felt all these years without her until just now.

He didn't want this to ever end.

He didn't want to live another day without having her in it. Nothing had changed, but he so fervently wanted it to.

Unable to hold back, pivoting on his elbows, Matt slid into her. He caught his breath, feeling her quicken around him as he entered.

Matt groaned, struggling to hold back for just a few more moments. He was determined to bring Natalie up with him, determined to have her share the moment. Because it had never been about self-satisfaction, not even the first time. It had always been about her, about them, about the magic they created together.

Feeling Natalie begin to frantically move beneath him, Matt locked into a rhythm, going faster and faster as the ever evolving sensation urged him on to race to the top of the mountain, then seized him in its grip.

He heard Natalie cry out his name, felt her arching beneath him to absorb every nuance of the climax he'd brought to her.

His heart surged.

With every fiber in his being, Matt struggled to prolong the feeling, to postpone, as long as humanly possible, the dizzying descent back to earth. And to reality.

But even as the euphoria began to softly loosen its hold on him and slip away, Matt held her tightly to him. Just glorying in the feel of her beside him.

"You tip every delivery boy this way?" he murmured the question against her temple, his lips brushing against her hair. "Because if you do, you might be onto something."

Her heart still hammering the last stanza of the "Anvil Chorus," Natalie turned her body into his. His playful mood was infectious. "I was a born-again virgin until just now."

One eyebrow arched as he looked at her quizzically. "Born-again virgin?"

That was the way she'd come to think of herself. "I haven't been with anyone in eight years. So I figured that pretty much qualifies me as a beginner if not born-again virgin altogether. So I figured…" She let her voice trail off as she shrugged.

The sound of Matt's laughter echoed around the room and brought a burst of sunshine into her soul. The way it always had in the past. There was something about the sound that lifted her spirits and coaxed a smile from her lips. Even on those occasions when she didn't think there was anything to smile about.

Matt laced his hands together around her shoulders, holding her close to him. Content to remain like that all night long. He didn't have to be anywhere until nine the next morning, and there was nowhere else he wanted to be than here.

"So where does this put us, other than the floor?"

She drew in a breath. This was where she could reclaim her dignity. But the only thing she resorted to was the truth.

"Nowhere," she answered. "I'm assuming that whatever made you leave is still there, still a reality that you're dealing with."

He thought of the phone call from his brother, the frantic one that demanded he "do something. Make it right." Those were always Scott's words when he asked—demanded really—that he come to his rescue. Pointing out that if Scott had behaved, if he'd kept his pants on to begin with, there'd be no need for his brother to put him on the spot and "make it right."

He'd resigned himself to the fact that Scott would always be Scott. A leopard whose spots didn't change with time.

But, like it or not, Scott was family. *His* family and he couldn't just stand by and let something happen to Scott, no matter how tempted he was to hit his older brother upside the head in hopes of knocking some kind of sense into him.

Not likely, Matt thought.

Scott's world revolved around Scott and no one else—until he feared retaliation because of some stupid transgression on his part. Like the time his brother bedded Candace.

"Yes," he told her quietly, "nothing changed."

She really was an idiot, wasn't she? And now Matt knew it as well as she did. Doing her damnedest to keep her tears in check, Natalie began to rise.

She was surprised when he wouldn't let her. Matt

tightened his hold on her, making her stay put. She raised her arm to push him away when he stopped her cold with his words.

It was time to tell her. He didn't want her imagination conjuring up false, negative theories, didn't want her believing something that wasn't true. Believing that he didn't love her. Natalie deserved to know the truth.

"You want to know why I left that morning?"

She stopped struggling. "Considering that I've asked you several times since yesterday, I'd say you just made a very clever leap to a conclusion."

Her sarcasm didn't affect him. He knew it was her shield, her way of keeping the pain at bay. Hopefully what he had to tell her would minimize the pain. "I left for you."

So he kept trying to tell her. "Oh, please." She rolled her eyes. He was more clever than that. "You're going to have to do better than that. That's right up there with that old saw, 'it's not you, it's me.'"

"It *was* me," he insisted, then amended. "Or more accurately, it was my family. And it still is my family. The morning I left, I'd gotten a call from Scott. He was in some kind of trouble—"

"What kind?" she asked.

"It doesn't matter. What mattered was I realized that he and the rest of them would always keep pulling me back in. I've tried to separate myself from my family, to go my own way and just pretend they didn't exist, but—"

"They're still your family," Natalie supplied with a sigh. How well she knew that feeling. There'd been a time when she'd considered changing her last name. But that still wouldn't change who she was, or that they were her family. "Welcome to *my* world." She propped herself up on her elbow and looked down at him. Was it as simple as that? He'd pulled away from her because of his family? "Look, if you can put up with mine, I can put up with yours."

There was one basic flaw with that philosophy. "Yours doesn't kill people. Doesn't have people after them because they want to 'even' some score. I left you because I couldn't put you in that kind of danger just because I couldn't live without you."

"Too late," she declared. "Candace's murder just changed the rules of the game. There might be a very good chance that my sister was killed because someone was looking to get even—" Natalie abruptly stopped, her eyes widening as she just now recalled the end of his statement. "Did you just say you couldn't live without me?"

Maybe he shouldn't have told her. But now that he had, he wasn't about to say that he hadn't meant what he'd said.

"Yes."

Feeling her heart beginning to accelerate, Natalie struggled to sound calm. "And how long has this been going on?"

He told her the simple truth. "Since the first moment I laid eyes on you."

If she was smart, she wouldn't believe him. But she'd already proven she wasn't smart. Because she was lying on her kitchen floor, naked—and wanting more.

Natalie laughed softly and shook her head as she moved closer to him. "You know, for a monk—" which was what he'd alluded his life was like "—you have a very smooth tongue." Each word was separated by a small, flittering kiss as her lips lightly grazed different parts of his anatomy. She felt him stiffening against her and smiled. "Encore?"

"I thought you'd never ask," he told her just before he brought her up to his level and sealed his mouth to hers.

Chapter 11

She was getting nowhere.

And the worst part about it, she was getting there in slow motion.

Natalie could feel her frustration mounting, governing her every waking moment—and keeping her from finding sleep for more than a few fitful minutes at a time.

Thanks to Matt's connections, over the last week she had been able to question anyone at the party who might have seen her twin interact with people at the gala. The upshot of that had been that, other than posing for the cameras and exchanging a few words with reporters, Candace hadn't really talked to anyone besides Luke Montgomery and Matt himself.

Matt, at least, didn't seem to have anything to hide. She wasn't all that sure about Luke yet.

Not only had Matt covertly gotten her a copy of the

tapes that her own department had commandeered but he had also given her Montgomery's guest list under the guise that it was public knowledge who had attended. For her part over this last week, Natalie had judiciously gone down that list, calling or going to see as many people on it as she physically could.

All she had managed to garner over and over again was not information but condolences. For the most part, once she identified herself as Candace's twin, the people she spoke with focused on the words "so sorry for your loss." When it came to saying something kind or flattering about Candace, there was far less enthusiasm. The kindest thing that anyone could offer was that her sister was "a woman who knew how to have a good time."

Natalie sincerely doubted that. What Candace had actually done was try desperately to numb herself, to party to the point of exhaustion. She'd gone at an almost frenzied pace from man to man in hopes of finding *the* man, never realizing that relationships did not spring out of the ground fully formed but actually took work. Constant work. With luck, that work made the relationship better. Made it golden.

Candace wasn't the only one to be disappointed, she thought now, sitting at her desk in the semidarkness in the room she used as her office.

That was the kind of relationship, eight years ago, she would have sworn she had with Matt. And yet, look how wrong she'd been about that. The first perceived bump in the road and he had vanished without a trace. Never mind that the bump originated with him and not her…and that he'd done it supposedly for selfless reasons. What it came down to in her mind was that he hadn't thought enough of her to ask how she felt about this sacrifice he was making. He hadn't even bothered to ask if she agreed with his reasoning.

If he had, she would have talked him out of it. Then. But now, there was no point in going over old ground. Too much time had passed, too many years of hurt that hadn't been remedied. Despite the lovemaking that first night—and the second and the third and all the rest that followed—the path they were on had been set. Try as she might, she didn't see them going off into the sunset together.

Besides, he hadn't said anything about getting together, not in any sort of permanent way. For the last week they *had* gotten together every evening to discuss their combined lack of headway in this investigation. Somehow these discussions always culminated with them going to bed together. Natalie mused that their insatiable desire for one another was most likely the result of an attraction that should have come with its own asbestos container because, left out in the open, it was as combustible as nitroglycerin.

So here she was, slipping out of her bed, padding in bare feet into the next room, dressed in a longer-than-usual-peasant blouse she'd pulled on and nothing more. Restless, her mind going in three different directions at once, Natalie wanted to look over her notes in order to see if there was something she'd somehow missed. Anything, no matter how tiny, that might finally send her off in the right direction.

She'd been at it less than twenty minutes when she became aware that she was no longer alone in the room. Matt had come up behind her.

The next moment, he lifted her hair away and pressed

a kiss to the back of her neck. "Bed's cold without you," he murmured.

His breath was warm on her skin, sending shivers down her spine.

"This is April in Vegas. Nothing is cold in Vegas in April." She struggled to sound coherent. She would've thought that after the torrid session they'd had together, she couldn't be aroused again so soon.

But she could and she was.

"Relatively cold compared to before," Matt amended. As he spoke, he placed his hands on her bare shoulders.

It was a possessive gesture she found oddly comforting. She never did think clearly around him, Natalie mused.

"Have a sudden inspiration?" he asked, looking over her shoulder at her notes.

With effort, she focused on what had drawn her out of bed.

"I wish." Natalie sighed. "I don't even know if Candace was killed and the ring was stolen to make it look like a robbery, or the ring was the object of the crime and she was killed when she wouldn't give it up."

"Does it matter?" There was an ironic tone to his voice and she knew what he meant. That either way, the outcome was that Candace was dead.

"It might help me figure out who did it," she explained. "If Candace picked up someone and brought them home, then that explains why the door wasn't jimmied and points to the killer being a stranger. If it was someone she knew, she opened the door because of that—and whoever killed her did it for personal reasons."

Matt took her argument a step further. "Maybe the 'personal' reasons was that he—or she," he inserted although it was obvious to Natalie that he really didn't think that a woman was responsible for Candace's death, "felt the ring actually should belong to them and not Candace."

That was an odd thing to say. "I thought the ring was always in our family."

"I heard a rumor to the contrary the other day."

Natalie was immediately intrigued. Swinging around to look up at him, her mouth dropped open. She hadn't realized that Matt hadn't put anything on when he'd come looking for her. Her present position put her at a definite disadvantage as far as clear thinking went. Clearing her throat, she rose from the chair, doing her best to keep her eyes on his.

"Why didn't you say anything earlier?" she wanted to know, her voice quavering just a little.

They'd gotten into it pretty hot and heavy almost from the moment he'd walked in the door. She'd been on his mind the entire day. By the time he'd come over, all he'd wanted to do was make love with her until he dropped from exhaustion.

"Earlier I was occupied," he told her.

No, she wasn't going to allow herself to get side-tracked. Not this time.

"This is important," she insisted, hitting his shoulder with the flat of her hand.

He merely grinned. "So was what I was doing earlier," he answered, before returning to the subject at hand. "Besides, it *was* only a rumor, and I hadn't heard anything to back it up."

Still, it was a new idea, a possible new direction to go in. "We need to follow that up."

She remembered the note her father had told her he'd gotten. A note that seemed to threaten all of them. She'd kept that little tidbit from Matt on the pretext that she didn't want him to worry. Now her father's fear had gotten legs.

"If someone thought the ring belonged to him, or was stolen from his family, well, that could be motive enough to kill Candace when she wouldn't surrender the ring—" She caught her breath as she felt Matt slip his hand up along her thigh. "What are you doing?"

"Sliding my fingers along the softest, most tempting piece of flesh I've ever had the good fortune to touch," he told her seductively.

Her pulse began to scramble. "I can't think when you do that."

"That's the whole idea," he admitted. Taking her hand, he began to draw her from the room. "Come back to bed, Natalie. It's three in the morning. The only people who are up at this hour are the gambling addicts and the pit crews who make their living off the addicts. We'll pursue this angle in the morning," he promised her. He pressed another kiss to her temple. "Right now, all I want to pursue is you."

Damn but he could reduce her to a quivering mound of jelly in an instant. "That would be assuming that I was on the run."

The grin on his lips grew wider—and all the sexier for it. He was already making love to her with his eyes. "Yeah."

She could feel the heat radiating from his body. Encompassing her. Making her yearn for contact. "I'm not running."

"Even better," he murmured, closing his arms around her and pulling her to him.

Damn it, she was supposed to be concentrating on finding Candace's killer, not surrendering to a man with whom she had one hell of a past and no obvious future.

What was she thinking?

That was just it, she wasn't thinking. She was feeling. Feeling an entire cauldron of emotions that were swirling madly through her.

And then, while her mouth was still sealed to his, she felt herself being lifted up in the air. Lifted and carried back to her bed.

The journey, punctuated with a myriad of hot, passionate, open-mouth kisses, was slow going. But half the fun, she knew, was in getting there.

By the time they did, he had her so worked up that she was all but ready to attack him.

The passion escalated to heights she didn't think could be achieved, especially with someone who knew her the way Matt did.

She knew that in the not-too-far distance, the inevitable waited. Matt would leave again, and she would let him go. Because he felt that ultimately they didn't belong together, and she had too much pride to beg him to reconsider.

But for now, they had this little piece of paradise together, and she was going to make the very most of it for as long as she possibly could. She knew she was living on borrowed time, and it made every moment that much sweeter, that much more precious.

Matt sat on the bed, watching Natalie get dressed, silently marveling that such a simple act could exude such poetry at the same time. "I could come with you, you know."

Natalie slipped on a pair of black pumps. Her entire outfit was as tasteful and subdued as Candace's had always been flamboyant and scintillating.

Her eyes met Matt's in the mirror above the bureau as she put in a pair of diamond studs.

"I know. But it's better all around if you don't." She was aware that the answer she'd given him wasn't the one Matt wanted to hear, even though he didn't challenge her on it. Feeling guilty because he was being so nice about it, she tried to explain. "Seeing you is going to remind my father that he owes your family money and—"

Natalie abruptly stopped talking. What she was saying was making Matt's point for him, or at least part of it. He'd told her that he felt they couldn't make a go of it because of their families. That his would always keep reeling him in. That, no matter what he did on his own, he would always be thought of as part of the Schaffer family, a family who had underworld ties and who poisoned everything it touched.

He hadn't wanted their reputation to touch her.

She'd stopped talking so suddenly, he thought something was wrong. Matt got up off the bed and crossed to her.

"What's the matter?"

"Nothing." She forced a smile to her lips in an effort

to convince him that everything was fine. "If you want to come to the memorial service, then come," she said, inviting him. And then she added, "I'd like that." Her eyes swept over him. He was dressed in the suit he'd worn last night. It was light gray with a dark blue shirt to set off his eyes. He looked much too vibrant for a memorial service. "Do you have a dark suit?" He gave her a look that all but said, *You have to be kidding.* "Okay, then," she decided out loud. "If you're serious about wanting to be with me, then yes, I'd love to have you at Candace's memorial service." She tried not to think about her father's reaction to seeing Matt there.

"Not that I'm trying to jinx this, but what just changed your mind?"

She gave him an innocent look as she spread her hands wide. "I'm female."

He laughed then and brushed a quick kiss against her lips. "Yeah, I noticed."

It took Matt less than a half hour to get ready, a fact that left her in more than a little awe, especially since part of that time included driving over to his place in order to change into a navy-blue suit.

"Approve?" he asked her as he got back into her vehicle.

"Approve," she replied with a nod and a smile. And so, she added silently, would every woman over the age of five and under the age of one hundred. If they had a pulse, they would definitely approve of the handsome man sitting beside her.

Her father, however, would be a different story. Driving to the small chapel on the cemetery grounds where the service was to be held, Natalie braced herself.

It had been years since she had sought or needed parental approval, but she still hated confrontations.

They weren't the first ones in the chapel. Her father and his wife, her stepsister and younger sister were already there.

She was aware of the looks she was getting from her family the moment she walked through the chapel doors with Matt walking beside her. Jenna's face registered first surprise, then looked pleased. Silver just looked stunned. Natalie was well aware that her famous stepsister was sizing up the man who was with her. Silver wasn't Candace, she didn't see every man as a possible key to happiness, but she made no secret of the fact that she did like a good, decent specimen of manhood when she saw one.

Daggers and hostile glares came her way courtesy of her father and his trophy wife. Most likely for different reasons, Natalie surmised, pretending not to notice either of them.

The minister she'd engaged for the service was at the podium. Their eyes met and Natalie nodded, giving him the signal to begin even though the chapel was only half full. She was well aware of the fact that Candace had so-called friends who thought that watches were a conspiracy by the government to entrap them in small, confining boxes that were dictated by the sweeping hands of a clock.

The upshot was that half of the "friends" she'd invited weren't here. She figured it was either because they'd forgotten the day, because they didn't want to acknowledge the fact that a life force like Candace was actually gone—or because they simply didn't care.

All Natalie knew for sure was that the bottom line was they weren't here and somewhere, wherever Candace was, she was disappointed at the relatively small showing.

Had she made this service public, Natalie was certain the paparazzi would have come out in force. That might have been enough to lure out the so-called friends who weren't here now.

Part of her almost felt that she should have done that. Because this was for Candace, not her. But in the end, she decided that her twin's life had been a three-ring circus for years and not in a good way. Her death shouldn't be allowed to follow that same path.

It was a short service.

When Natalie delivered the eulogy, she tried very hard to concentrate on only the good moments and spoke, for the most part, about Candace's generous heart when they were growing up together. It was a life, she concluded, cut short much too soon because she wanted to believe that the best was yet to come for Candace.

Afterward, a few of her friends spoke, saying they would miss her at parties and that she left very big shoes to fill. There was not much to say after that. Natalie was painfully aware that her father said nothing. At one point, he looked as if he was about to stand up, but Rebecca Lynn had linked her arm through his, even while they were seated, and she restrained him from rising. With a shrug, he remained where he was.

As the participants filed by the minister on their way out of the small church, Natalie realized that her father had brought his housekeeper with him. It was she who was in charge of Candace's two children. With a boy tethered to each hand, the woman managed to keep the boys in check. Mick and David looked oddly subdued, as if they understood what was happening.

In her heart, she sincerely hoped not. Funerals and memorial services were no place for children. Natalie noticed that her half brother was mercifully missing from the service.

Bending down, Natalie looked from one boy to the other. She smiled at them. "You guys okay?" she asked, doing her best to sound upbeat.

Two mop-heads bobbed up and down as they mumbled, "Uh-huh."

What was going to become of them? she wondered. She doubted that her father was going to allow the boys to move in with him and that would mainly be the fault of the empty-headed witch of the west. Rebecca Lynn would not welcome children who were not her own.

She was tempted to claim the boys herself, but she was realistic. Because of the nature of her work, she knew she wouldn't be allowed to take them in or adopt them. The job called her away at odd times of the night and day. It was certainly not the most stable environment for two little boys.

But there was time enough to worry about that later, she told herself. Rising to her feet again, she slanted a glance toward Matt. For now, she had more than enough on her plate.

"May I see you for a moment, Natalie?" her father requested, his voice taking on that formal tone that, as a child, used to tell her that she was in trouble.

She turned to Matt. "I'll only be a minute," she

promised. He nodded and stepped back, after saying, "Sorry for your loss, Mr. Rothchild."

Harold made no acknowledgment that he even heard him speak. "What were you thinking?" her father demanded the moment Matt stepped away.

She was still angry at him for not getting up to say something, however small, in tribute to Candace. For God's sake, his daughter was dead. Didn't he care?

"You're going to have to be more specific than that, Dad."

"You know perfectly well what I'm referring to," Harold insisted peevishly. He looked at Matt. "How could you bring Schaffer here with you?"

It was on the tip of her tongue to say, "My arrangements, my choice," but that would put her in the same low class as Rebecca Lynn, so she focused only on addressing his question. "Because he said he wanted to pay his respects to Candace."

"Respects, huh." Harold blew out an angry breath. "The bastard just wants to keep tabs on me."

"I'm sure if that's what he has in mind, Dad, he would see a reason to have to do it at a memorial service," she mocked. Turning serious, she added, "Come on, now. I really doubt that this would be the place he'd plan on a confrontation. Besides," she reminded her father, "you said you owe money to his family, not to him."

A harsh laugh escaped his lips. "Same thing."

"No," she said firmly, thinking of how she related to her own family and their actions; they might share the same last name, but they were *not* one and the same. "They're not."

Chapter 12

When the memorial service was finally over and Candace's ashes had been placed inside the family mausoleum at the cemetery, Natalie was more than ready to put the whole ordeal behind her. Being around her family for any length of time always managed to exhaust her emotionally if not physically.

Not to mention the fact that the sadness had finally really hit her.

Candace was dead.

All of her life, she had always been accustomed to being one half of a whole. That was just the way things were. She and Candace hadn't been identical, but there was no denying that there was still an indelible bond. Even when she didn't see Candace for months at a stretch—other than the usual tabloid in-your-face stories that periodically featured her twin—she knew Candace was out there somewhere. Breathing. Doing. Being her other half.

Now that was gone, and she was no longer part of a set. She had to rethink her existence. Become accustomed to thinking of herself in the singular.

It was an odd, odd feeling. She sincerely doubted that anyone who had never lost a twin would understand, but there was this acute feeling of being lost, of something missing.

Almost, she thought ruefully, slanting a covert look toward Matt, like the feeling she'd had when she'd woken up that fateful morning and realized that he had left her for good.

She supposed that maybe that was her fate in life. To be left behind. Granted that Candace, as self-centered as her twin could sometimes be, hadn't any control over severing their tie.

But Matt had.

As for now, there was no doubt in Natalie's mind that, as fantastic as the lovemaking was, Matt was only here temporarily. He'd told her about being based in Los Angeles, and she knew that whenever whatever it was he was attending to for Montgomery was over, Matt would be on the next plane bound for L.A. and out of her life.

Again.

She couldn't dwell on that now, Natalie told herself, couldn't fixate on what was to be. She could only live in the moment.

That, and find Candace's killer, no matter what it took.

"You're awfully quiet," Matt commented as he escorted her out of the mausoleum. Outside, the sun seemed particularly bright and the weather oppressively hot for that time of year.

Natalie stripped off her suit jacket. The sleeveless black-and-white silk blouse felt as if it was sticking to her spine. "Just thinking."

It wasn't a stretch to guess who she was thinking about. He couldn't remember Natalie ever looking this sad before.

"About Candace?"

And you. But there was no point in mentioning that, so she merely nodded. "Yes."

Compassion filled him. "I know what it's like to lose somebody." He didn't seem aware of the quiet sigh he uttered before continuing. "It's the kind of grief that sticks with you. Eventually, you make peace with it and go on, but it's always there, somewhere in the shadows, no matter how small and manageable you think it's ultimately become."

Natalie stopped walking and looked at him. He sounded as if he was talking about someone he'd loved. Had Matt found someone else after he'd left her after all?

Of course he had, you idiot, she mocked herself. Eight years was a long time for a virile man like Matt to do without female companionship. He hadn't been that self-contained monk she'd imagined.

A tiny sprig of jealousy sprang up inside her chest. With concentrated effort, she yanked it out by the roots. What was the matter with her? She was an independent woman. Her *own* person, not some moonstruck young girl—the way she had once been.

Her voice gave none of her feelings away as she asked, "Who did you lose?"

To be honest, she half expected Matt to shrug off her question, or at the very least, to change the subject. But instead he answered her.

"The only one I was ever close to in my family, my mother, Amy. The most selfless woman to ever walk the face of the earth. Even on her deathbed, she wasn't thinking about herself, but of the family." He sighed heavily. "She asked me to watch out for my older brother. Scott always had a tendency to get himself into situations that he couldn't get out of."

She heard the sadness in his voice. He was serious. "Your mother?" she repeated.

"Yes." He noted the surprised look on her face. "What did you think I was going to say?"

She lifted her shoulders in a half shrug. "Some unforgettable love of your life."

He looked at her for a long moment. "There's only been one." His tone of voice left no room for doubt. "There's only one chance at the brass ring in this life," he told her solemnly, taking her arm and continuing to walk. "If you're lucky, you get it. If you're not…" His voice trailed off, leaving it to her to fill in the blank.

They had almost left the cemetery grounds and Rothchild mausoleum, where her paternal grandparents and her mother were said to be buried, when she noticed him. Had he been there all the time? At the chapel and then at the cemetery? How had she missed him?

"Conner?"

When Matt looked over toward the person she had called out to, Natalie felt him stiffening at her side. "If you want to have a word with him, I'll wait for you by the car," Matt offered, his tone almost formal.

The suggestion caught her off guard. "You don't have to go, Matt," she told him even as Conner was approaching them.

Matt shook his head. "Better this way," was all he said as he retreated, then turned on his heel and walked away.

There was obviously no love lost between the two men, she thought. A lot of that going around, she mused.

Her cousin, Conner Rothchild, was a defense attorney for the family's large, prestigious legal firm: Rothchild, Rothchild & Bennigan. Tall, with hazel eyes and dark brown hair, the thirty-three-year-old lawyer was the older son of her father's younger brother, Michael. Though Michael Rothchild was a brilliant attorney in his own right, it was obvious to the family that he resented Harold and felt as if he could never crawl out from beneath his older brother's shadow.

Lots of discord in this family, she thought sadly just as Conner reached her side.

"Hello, Conner," she greeted him politely, deliberately dispensing with the obligatory air kiss that was so popular among the rich and famous. "I didn't see you in the church," she confessed.

"You had a lot to deal with," he countered. "And I was in the back. I came late. I wasn't really sure how Uncle Harold would react to my attending the service. You either," he added with a smile that always had her guessing as to its genuineness.

But that was mainly because they had grown up as adversaries, thanks to the efforts of both their fathers. Until Ricky's birth five years ago, Uncle Michael enjoyed rubbing her father's nose in the fact that he had only females in his family while he, Michael, had fathered two strong, strapping sons: Conner and Michael Jr. The implication was not lost on her. To Uncle Michael, women were second-class citizens.

She remembered always feeling as if the family gatherings they had were merely excuses for some sort of competitive comparison. Birthdays, Christmas, Thanksgiving, it didn't matter. The agenda was always the same. Each brother tried to top the other, and neither was above using their offspring and pitting them against one another like some human form of cockfighting.

Time and again, she could remember being played against Conner and his brother. The competition turned more serious as they grew up. Then it was accomplishment against accomplishment, career against career. More than once, the criminals she had arrested wound up being put back on the street, thanks to the efforts of Conner and her uncle.

"You're welcome here," she replied tersely. "It's a memorial service, not one of those family competitions we were all forced to endure."

He made no comment about that, or the use of the word *forced.* He'd been born competitive and loved nothing better than winning. Competitions, to his way of thinking, kept you sharp and on your toes. And the world belonged to the winners, not the losers.

He put on his best somber face. Was he acting? Natalie wondered. "I was sorry to hear about Candace. Do the police know who did it?"

He was pumping her, wasn't he? She wasn't about to give him the satisfaction of sharing any information. "It's too soon to tell."

"How about Schaffer?" Conner nodded toward Matt in the distance. The latter stood waiting beside his car at the curb. "Anyone look into where he was the night in question?" he asked. Then, before she could respond, he commented, "Pretty brazen of Schaffer coming here like this."

There was that protective feeling again, she thought. "And why is that?"

Hazel eyes shifted to her face. "Don't play dumb, Natalie. It doesn't become you. Everyone knows your father and Schaffer's people are connected, but it wasn't a match made in heaven. More like something that the devil had a hand in orchestrating." He laughed shortly. "I figure that Matt's just like the rest of them." He grew more sober as he added, "Don't turn your back on him, Natalie."

Since when did Conner care what she or any of her side of the family did or didn't do? "Your concern is touching."

If he was aware of the sarcasm, he didn't show it. "You are my cousin," Conner pointed out. "Little amusing rivalries aside, I wouldn't want to see anything happening to you." And then he shrugged, as if he knew that his words were being deflected and that she didn't believe him. "But you'll do what you want. You were always headstrong that way." He paused, as if debating adding anything. And then he did. "Just be careful," he warned again.

"I'm a cop," she told him. "I'm always careful. I have to be," she added. "Especially since you managed to put so many of the people with grudges against me back on the street."

"The cases were weak," he pointed out. "And remember, innocent until proven guilty."

Others might buy into her cousin's charm, but she didn't. She was immune to it. "Or their money runs out, whichever happens first."

Conner didn't bother contradicting her. He actually looked as if he was amused by her rejoinder. And then he took his leave. "Hope the next time I see you, it'll be under happier circumstances."

She nodded, then, just as he was turning to go, she decided to ask Conner one question.

"Where's Uncle Michael?" She knew her other cousin, Michael Jr., was out of town on business, but Candace had been her uncle's niece. She would have thought that he would have put aside any differences, petty or otherwise, that he had with her father and attend the service. Natalie knew she'd sent him an invitation.

"Home," Conner confessed, and she saw that he wasn't entirely comfortable with what he was telling her. "Funerals depress him. He likes to avoid them whenever he can."

"Obviously, he thought he could," she concluded with a sigh. Maybe it was better this way after all. Maybe the sight of his younger brother would only further upset her father. "I'd like to say it's nice seeing you again, Conner, but, well, you know…"

For a moment, they were on the same wavelength and her cousin seemed compassionate. She knew better than to think it might continue.

"Yeah, I know," he answered. "Well, take care of

yourself, Nat." And with that, Conner turned away and walked off in the opposite direction, where he'd parked his car.

Matt came to attention and dropped his arms to his sides as he saw Natalie part ways with Conner and begin to head toward him. He waited until she was only a few feet away before he asked, "So what did your cousin have to say?"

She couldn't help wondering if Conner had come out of a sense of obligation, because no one else from his side of the family had attended—or if there was another reason for his presence. Her suspicious mind was due in part to her job description and in part because of her family background. Hardly anyone did something for no reason at all.

"Why?" she asked, stopping at the curb. "Were your ears burning?"

Matt looked mildly surprised. "Your cousin didn't have anything better to do than talk about me?" He held the passenger-side door open for her.

Independent or not, she had to admit she liked encountering touches of chivalry. And if nothing else, Matt knew how to treat a woman like a lady. Surrendering a smile, Natalie got into the car.

"Not talk about you so much as warn me about you," she corrected.

He'd just rounded the hood and was getting in himself. He stopped mid-motion, then slid in behind the wheel. "Warn you?" What the hell was Rothchild warning her about?

"Uh-huh." Pulling on the shoulder strap, she fastened

her seat belt securely. "Seems that he thinks you might have an ulterior motive for being here. Or at least that you have some kind of an agenda."

His first comment was drowned out by the sound of the engine turning over. She had a hunch that maybe it was better that way.

"We all have agendas," Matt told her as he pulled away from the curb and wove his way into the flow of traffic. "Mine is keeping you safe."

It had been a very long time since anyone had even pretended to take care of her. "Excuse me?"

"Just in case this does involve some kind of a vendetta." He couldn't tell if his answer offended her sense of independence. To be honest, he didn't much care. What he did care about was making sure nothing happened to her. But, to keep the peace, he explained himself. "You'll have to forgive me, but that's the kind of culture that I grew up in. Vendettas and paybacks. If that is the case, you're going to need someone watching your back."

"I'm a police detective," she once again reminded him. "I can watch my own back. Besides," she reasoned, "I'm practically estranged from my family and I am *so* not like a Rothchild. Why in heaven's name would I be in any kind of 'danger'—assuming there's a shred of truth in this theory of yours?"

He didn't bother telling her that he had a gut feeling about this. That there was more to this ring business than Harold was telling her and that, for some reason, it had cost Candace her life. What he did was try to spell it out in neutral terms.

"Because, if it does involve revenge, whoever is responsible most likely is not your garden-variety rocket scientist who has carefully thought this all out. Most people who seek revenge are driven by emotions, not logic." And that Matt knew for a fact. If growing up a Schaffer had taught him nothing else, it had taught him that.

Her suspicions were aroused. Natalie studied his face closely as she asked, "Do you know something I don't?"

Actually, there was one piece of information he did have that she didn't, but he wanted to look into it a little more before sharing, so when he answered her, it was in the negative.

"No," he confessed. "I'm just spinning theories and trying to take everything under consideration."

She was quiet for a moment as she digested what he was saying. Something didn't quite fit.

"Not that I don't appreciate the help. After all, I was the one who initially dragged you into this." As with a suspect she was questioning, Natalie moved in for the so-called kill. In this case, it was his motives she was after. "But when did you suddenly become so dedicated to finding Candace's killer?"

"The first time I made love with you." He saw her brow furrow in confusion and realized his mistake. "The second first time," he corrected. "Meaning this time around, not eight years ago."

"I know what that means," she interrupted, then asked, "And that's the only reason?"

"Yeah." Taking a right turn, he glanced at his watch. It was getting late. "Mind if I drop you off at your place? I only took a few hours off, and Luke's expecting me at the casino for a meeting at one." It was close to that now.

"I don't mind you dropping me off," she told him

agreeably, then added, "but make it The Janus instead of my place."

Matt was immediately suspicious. She'd already put in a great deal of time there. "Why?"

"Why don't you leave that up to me?" *Because if I tell you, you'll give me an argument, and I don't feel up to arguing.*

He looked at her incredulously just as he squeaked through a yellow light that was about to turn red. "You still don't trust me? What is it that Conner said to you?" It couldn't have been just an ambiguous warning. There had to be something more to it, he reasoned.

But Natalie waved her hand at his question. "Conner doesn't matter. I'm never sure about anything he says," she admitted. Her cousin was very capable of lying to put her on the wrong trail for his own reasons. She didn't have time or the inclination to try to unravel why he was warning her about Matt. "We weren't exactly encouraged to have a close, honest relationship as kids. We were always being pitted against one another, and he liked winning far too much for my taste. As a matter of fact, he still does."

"You still haven't answered my first question," Matt persisted. This time, when the light flashed yellow, he stepped on the brake so he could look at her. People had trouble lying if they were looked at head-on. Decent people, at any rate. "You don't trust me?"

"It's not a matter of trust," she insisted. He wasn't going to give up, she could see that. Natalie decided to give him just a little and hoped that would satisfy him. "If I told you why, then I'd be involving you and you might have to pick sides. I don't want to put you in that position."

When had this happened? "It didn't seem to matter to you a week ago."

"That was a week ago." Why couldn't he just let things be? She waved her hand at the road before them. "Stop acting like some two-bit private investigator and just drive, okay?"

"Okay. I'll take you to The Janus," he conceded. "And I won't ask any questions." *For now,* he added silently. Sparing her a glance, he told her, "You're going to look out of place in that outfit."

Unlike Candace, who had always been very particular about her clothes, insisting on only the latest fashions and the most expensive designers, Natalie could care less about her so-called image. She merely shrugged at his observation.

"Won't be the first time. Won't be the last."

"Suit yourself," he told her. But if she thought that he wasn't going to try to find out what she was up to, she really didn't know him anymore.

Her answer was self-assured. "Thanks, but I usually do."

He smiled to himself as he pressed his foot down on the accelerator. That she didn't have to tell him. "Yeah, I remember."

Chapter 13

With the gala tapes she'd viewed all but burned into her brain, Natalie's main reason for returning to The Janus was to retrace her sister's steps that night as closely as possible. By trying to see things from Candace's line of vision, she was really hoping that something might strike her that hadn't previously.

Nothing did.

The case was getting colder, and though some crimes were solved months, even years after they'd taken place—often by accident after an incredible amount of man-hours had been put into the endeavor—most cases were either solved in the first seventy-two hours or forever remained open.

Natalie was aware that it had already been longer than that, but she absolutely refused to have her sister's murder fall into that black hole known as cold cases. If she had to take a leave of absence, she would, but she planned to devote herself to solving this crime if it was the last thing she did.

Matt hadn't lied to her when he told Natalie that he needed to get back to The Janus for a meeting, one that hinged not only on his attendance but on his delivering a report to his employer. It concerned the overall present state of security not just in the casino itself but in the hotel and the surrounding grounds as well. However, the moment his meeting with Montgomery was over, Matt quickly returned to his office.

He not only closed the door but he locked it and shut the blinds as well. He didn't want to take a chance on anyone walking in on him while he was on his private line.

Something regarding the missing ring had come to his attention late last night, and he wanted to verify the information before mentioning it to Natalie. The fastest way he knew how to get started was calling in one of the many favors that he was owed. Even so, part of him loathed doing it.

Because even if it was calling in a favor that was owed him, it theoretically placed him in debt to the person who was reciprocating the favor. And that person belonged to the Schaffer family network.

To say he disliked dealing with any of them was an understatement—he spent most of his time trying to disentangle himself from their vast tentacles. But in this case, it was the only way to proceed.

Besides, he told himself, he was doing this for Natalie.

And maybe, he thought as he listened to the phone on the other end ring, he was also doing it for

Candace. He and Natalie's twin had never gotten intimate the way Natalie had suggested, but, if he was being honest, he felt sorry for the dead woman. In a lot of ways, Candace had reminded him of a female version of his brother: a perpetual screwup unconsciously hunting for approval. And always hunting in all the wrong places.

Was that what had happened the last night of her life? Was the person Candace had hoped would light up her world responsible for bringing an end to it instead?

The ringing stopped. A husky voice, laced with the ragged remnants of sleep, came on the other end of the line. Matt glanced at his watch. It was close to two o'clock. But then, his cousin Vinnie was a player, and players in Vegas rarely ever got up until the sun went down.

"Whoever this is, you'd better have a damn good reason for waking me up," Vinnie growled, a snarling bear prematurely dragged out of hibernation.

"Vinnie, it's Matt," he began, then paused to let the name sink in.

True to form, his cousin wasn't processing information yet. "Matt?"

"Matt Schaffer. Your cousin. Scott's brother." Pausing between each sentence, Matt went down the line of several more filial connections they shared before finally saying, "The guy who saved your butt when the police were ready to haul you off to jail for that burglary they thought you'd committed."

The incident had turned out to be a case of mistaken identity and, at his aunt's tearful behest, he'd flown into Vegas to see what he could do to help her son. He'd stayed in Vegas less than three days that time. But even so, he'd been ever aware of the possibility that his path would cross Natalie's. That time, it hadn't.

He remembered smothering a kernel of disappointment as he flew back to L.A.

"Oh, *Matt,*" Vinnie cried as if his brain had suddenly kicked in. "How the hell are you? Still in L.A.?"

Matt leaned back in his chair. This might be slow going. "No, I'm here in Vegas."

"Vegas? Hell, you gotta let me have a chance to pay you back for what you did for me, man. Where're you staying?" Matt heard rustling on the other end, as if his cousin was hunting for his clothes. "I can swing by and pick—"

He stopped him before Vinnie could work up a full head of steam. "That's not necessary, Vinnie. But if you really want to pay me back, I do need a little information."

"Hey, you got it. My brain's your brain. Ask me," Vinnie invited, sounding eager to get out from under the weight of owing a debt.

Matt decided that he was going to have to give Vinnie a little background. Otherwise there were going to be endless questions.

"You know about that Rothchild woman who was found dead in her condo the other week?" With Vinnie, he took nothing for granted. Vinnie was generally oblivious to the outside world. He'd once gone an entire year before realizing that the price of postage had gone up.

This time, however, Vinnie was on top of things. "Yeah. Candace. A real party girl. We're really going to miss her around here." He almost sounded sad. "Damn waste if you ask me."

Matt paused, wanting to phrase his question just

right. He didn't want his cousin thinking that what he was asking would get back to the police. Any hint of the police would have Vinnie clamming up as if he'd swallowed a mouthful of crazy glue.

"According to the paper, they think she was wearing that big diamond ring." He played dumb. "Tears of the Quetzal I think the thing is called."

He heard his cousin's high-pitched laugh and remembered how grating a sound that could be. "Hell of a name, isn't it? I can't even pronounce it. Neither could Aunt Lydia."

Aunt Lydia. If he remembered his family dynamics, Aunt Lydia belonged to his mother's side of the family, once removed.

Matt smiled to himself. Maybe this was going to be easier than he'd initially thought. Just before he'd gotten together with Natalie last night, he'd become aware there was a rumor that had once made the rounds that the ring in question had fallen into the hands of his family for a while. If that was the case, then maybe someone in the family thought it should be returned. The members of his far-flung clan and their associates were capable of anything.

"Why would Aunt Lydia need to pronounce it?" Matt asked his cousin, trying to come across as only mildly curious.

Fully awake now, Vinnie cackled. "'Cause the crazy old lady claimed that the ring was hers. Said she 'found' it next to her dinner plate one evening when she was on this cruise down to Mexico. The same so-called cruise that Harold Rothchild supposedly whisked her off to when he was in-between wives," Vinnie added for good measure. It was obvious that he believed none of what Aunt Lydia had said.

This probably wasn't going to lead to anything, but since he had Vinnie on the phone, he wanted to hear whatever details his cousin had.

"Which wives?"

He'd obviously amused Vinnie. This time when his cousin laughed, Matt held the phone away from his ear until the noise stopped.

"Good question. Some guys never learn, do they?" Vinnie marveled, going off on a tangent. "His first wife croaks, and instead of being glad he was free, the damn fool starts looking around for another wife." Matt cleared his throat, and Vinnie got back on track. "But to answer your question, it was after his first one died and before he married the second one. Anna something-or-other I think. Anyway, that's the story Aunt Lydia tells."

Well, at least it was a starting point, Matt thought. Better than nothing. Everyone knew that Lydia Silecchia was several sandwiches short of a picnic basket. Maybe she had seen Candace flashing her ring on TV on one of those entertainment programs that made a point of recording every breath a celebrity took and decided to confront Natalie's sister.

Matt frowned. He knew this was a damn long shot, but right now, it was the only lead he had to go on so he might as well pursue it. With luck, it might actually lead him to something that made more sense.

Since there didn't seem to be any more information forthcoming, Matt decided to end the conversation before Vinnie got off track again. "Thanks, Vinnie, you've been a big help."

"Hey, what about us two studs getting together and having our way with the Vegas female population? You can be my wingman."

Aunt Lydia wasn't the only one who was delusional, Matt thought. "I'll get back to you on that," he promised, breaking the connection before Vinnie could say anything else. He replaced the receiver just as he heard a knock on his door. Now what? He was hoping to be able to go find Natalie, but that obviously was going to have to wait.

"Come in," he called out. When whoever was on the other side rattled the doorknob, Matt remembered that he'd locked the door. Not something he normally did. "Be right there."

Flipping the lock, he opened the door and found himself looking down at a very frustrated-looking Natalie. Her afternoon hadn't gone very well, he surmised.

"I just wanted to let you know I was leaving," she told him.

"I take it that whatever you were trying to do didn't pan out?"

She didn't feel like going into detail. "Something like that."

Matt glanced back at his desk. There was nothing going on that needed his immediate attention. He made a quick decision. "Want to go for a ride?"

There were times when she actually enjoyed cruising the more colorful streets of the strip, but she really wasn't in the mood this afternoon.

She shook her head. "Maybe some other—" And then Natalie stopped. The look on Matt's face told her that this was more than just a careless invitation to go for a drive. Did he find something out? She didn't bother containing the surge of excitement that entered her voice. "What's up?"

He didn't want her getting her hopes up too much. "Maybe nothing," he cautioned.

She knew Matt. He wouldn't have mentioned anything unless he was at least partially sure there was something to it. "And maybe something?" she countered.

He allowed a smile to curve the corners of his mouth. "Maybe."

She realized that they were walking out of his office and he had taken her arm. "Damn it, Matt, tell me. Why am I going on a ride with you?"

"Because you'll enjoy it?" He couldn't resist teasing.

That would have worked eight years ago. A lot of things would have worked eight years ago. But she'd done a lot of growing in that time. And a lot of hardening as well.

"What I don't enjoy is being in the dark."

"Oh, I don't know." His warm smile wove its way into her gut despite her efforts to block it. "Being in the dark has its advantages. As long as it's with the right person."

She studied his face. He wasn't just teasing her. There was something to all this. "You're on to something, aren't you?"

He looked at her for a long moment, his mind going places it had no business going. Because nothing had changed from last night, or the nights that had come before that. Nights they had spent making love and keeping the world at bay. He was still a different man than he had been when he had originally left Vegas— and her. A different man who, for better or worse, was set in his ways.

And she still deserved better.

"Yeah, I might be," he admitted, then cautioned, "But this still might be nothing."

She had never liked riddles, never enjoyed searching for puzzle pieces. She always wanted all the pieces out in the open, where she could see them.

"I swear, if you don't start giving me some tangible details I'm not going to be responsible for what I do to you, Matt."

"I heard that that ring of yours—"

She immediately interrupted him. He needed to get this straight. She had absolutely no interest in finding the ring. Her only interest in it was how it figured into her sister's death.

"My father's ring," Natalie corrected with feeling. "It's not my ring. It's my father's. And I don't care what he does with it."

And if Candace had felt the same way, she would probably still be alive, Natalie thought sadly.

"Sorry, your father's ring. Anyway, I came across a rumor that my family might have had possession of it for a while. If so, knowing my family, maybe someone decided that they should get it back."

They were crossing the casino floor, approaching the slot machines by the entrance, and Natalie stopped walking. "Your family?" she echoed, stunned. "That's a new one on me." She laughed dryly, shaking her head. It amazed her how much she still didn't know about what went on in her family. "But then, my father has never been exactly forthcoming about the diamond." *Or anything else,* she added silently.

"I'm not even sure just how he got hold of it. Supposedly my grandfather found it in his mines in Mexico, but that's never been verified. For all I know, Grandpa might have stolen it from someone." Even as she said it out loud, it made sense to her. "Joseph Rothchild wasn't exactly a man whose background could stand close investigation."

She resumed walking. The electronic doors opened wide for them. "So where is it exactly that we're going?" she wanted to know.

He nodded toward the closest valet. No words needed to be exchanged. The young man immediately went to retrieve Matt's sports car. "To see my Aunt Lydia."

More surprises, she thought, turning to look at Matt. "You have an Aunt Lydia?" He nodded in response. "You never mentioned her," she pointed out.

But then, when they'd been together all those years ago, they'd been wildly in love and very much into one another. Family history hardly mattered. In fact, she'd naively thought of them as being one another's families. Showed how much she knew.

"I never mentioned a lot of people in my family," he told her. And there was good reason for that. "I figured that the less you knew, the better off you were. Besides," he sighed, "it's not as if I was exactly thrilled about them."

Some were harmless and some even he was better off not knowing. When he was in his late teens and early twenties, it had been exciting, being part of an underground world. But then he grew up and the allure of that way of life quickly faded.

A lot of his relatives who were older than he was never grew up.

"Does your Aunt Lydia know who might have actually had the ring?" Natalie asked.

The valet arrived with his vehicle. Getting out, the valet—Skip according to his name tag—surrendered the keys to Matt and raced around to the other side to hold the passenger door open for Natalie.

"Aunt Lydia's the one who claims to have had the ring," Matt told her as he got in behind the steering wheel.

His sports car purred to life as Natalie's mouth dropped open. "Oh." And then she smiled as they sped away. It would have taken her a while to unearth this piece of information. "You know, sometimes you're a handy man to have around."

"Sometimes," he agreed.

When Lydia Silecchia had been a young girl, she dreamed of being a glamorous movie star. But several forays into little theater groups and a handful of some rather nasty reviews had her abandoning that world after a couple of years. Instead, she became a Vegas showgirl, ever on the lookout for a high roller who could give her the kind of life she longed for.

When she married Carlo Silecchia, he'd promised—and placed—the world at her feet. She hadn't known at the time that the world was on loan and that he was but a struggling underling in a long, winding chain that made up the Schaffer family structure. The American sounding name "Schaffer" having been adopted by Giovanni Scarpetta when he originally stepped off the boat at Ellis Island several generations ago.

Life for Lydia became a series of disappointments. So much so that she felt it necessary for her vivid imagination to fill in a few blanks in order for her to survive these shortfalls that life—and her husband—kept serving up. Her fantasies included building up her husband's importance in the world he labored in until, eventually, Lydia envisioned herself as the wife of a Don much like the celebrated one she'd seen in *The Godfather*. Whenever her own life lacked the drama she craved, she improvised.

How much she improvised became apparent to Natalie within the first ten minutes of their visit. Now a widow, living in a small, cluttered apartment on the good graces of "the family," which prided itself on taking care of its own, Lydia came to greet them wearing a floor-length electric-blue caftan that allowed her to sweep about the room like an anorexic Joan Crawford.

"Yes, the Tears of the Quetzal was mine. Beautiful, beautiful," she declared, her eyes getting a faraway look. "Never saw anything as beautiful as that ring," Lydia swore wistfully.

"What happened to it, Aunt Lydia?" Matt asked politely.

She lifted her bony shoulders, then let them fall again, and it was unclear if she was indicating that she didn't know or that what had happened to the ring was no longer of overwhelming consequence.

It turned out to be neither as she began to explain. "Strange things started happening soon after Harold gave me the ring."

"He gave it to you?" Natalie questioned. There wasn't the remotest chance that this was true. She knew that Rebecca Lynn had tried to wrest the ring away from him so she could show it off, and he had refused.

"I found it by my dinner plate one evening, during our Mediterranean cruise, but I knew it was from him," she said, a smug little smile on her face. "But, as I said, strange things started happening soon after I got the ring."

"Strange things?" Natalie coaxed when the woman's voice had trailed off along with her gaze.

"Yes. Horrible things. My son was shot. I lost money in investments. That ring *was* cursed, just like they said it was." She lifted her chin dramatically. "So I threw it away."

Matt looked at her, stunned that she would say something so absurd. "You did what?"

"I threw it away," Lydia repeated with a toss of her head, sending thin strands of impossibly blond hair flying over her shoulder. "I waited until everyone was asleep, then walked out onto the deck, stood right at the bow of the ship and threw the damn thing right into the ocean."

Natalie exchanged looks with Matt. His aunt was describing a scene from the end of *Titanic*.

"You went on another cruise to throw the ring away?" Matt asked.

Lydia looked a little confused for a moment, as if she hadn't realized that the ring had to have been in her possession for a little while in order for the "horrible things" to have happened.

"Yes. Yes, I did," Lydia said emphatically.

"I see." Matt stood up. Natalie was quick to join him. "Well, thank you for your time, Aunt Lydia."

"Don't mention it." She regally led the way to the front door of her small, memorabilia-crowded apartment. "I must say you took that a lot better than Anthony did."

"Anthony?" Natalie questioned. She looked to Matt for an explanation.

"Another cousin. Aunt Lydia's nephew," Matt filled in.

"I'm going to have to start keeping a scorecard to keep all the names straight," Natalie murmured under her breath. She caught the flash of a quick grin on Matt's face.

But Lydia hadn't heard the comment. She was too busy spinning her story and enjoying being the center of attention for a change. No one came to visit her anymore. "Anthony got real nasty. He said I had no right to do that. That the ring belonged to us. That we could have been rich if I hadn't lost it."

"Lost it?" Matt repeated innocently. "I thought you said you threw it away."

Lydia looked annoyed that he seemed to be trying to trip her up. "I lost it by throwing it away. Aren't you listening? I lost it and then she found it."

"She?" Natalie repeated, even as she wondered if anything this woman was saying was actually true. Was there someone else involved? Someone who might actually have once had the ring and for some reason, lost it to her father? Someone who'd gone to great lengths to get it back? "Who are you talking about?" she pressed, trying not to sound too eager.

Lydia's face puckered into a deep frown. "That blond tart. The one who likes to wiggle her body all the time. I saw her waving her hand at the camera. *She had on my ring,*" Lydia insisted. "Just ask Anthony. He saw it, too."

Chapter 14

That blond tart.

Natalie's heart quickened. Matt's aunt was talking about Candace. Had this delusional woman actually been instrumental in Candace's death by pointing out the ring to Anthony Silecchia?

Matt asked Lydia the question before she could. "You pointed the ring out to Anthony and said that it was yours?"

Lydia's expression became impatient. When she answered, it was as if she was talking to someone who was slow. "Yeah, well, he was in the room when that show that talks about celebrities was on." Impatience melted into annoyance, but it was aimed at Anthony. "He came by to ask to borrow some money. Like I had any," she sneered. "I told him all the money I coulda had was on that snooty broad's finger."

Her eyes narrowed as the thought seemed to strike

her for the first time. Matt could almost see the rusty wheels turning. "He seemed pretty interested in that ring. Got real quiet, then left right after the show was over." She ended her story in a whisper, as if she was telling the details to herself.

Maybe they finally *were* on to something. "Where is Anthony staying these days?" Matt asked.

Lydia waved her thin, veined hand around vaguely. She avoided his eyes as she said, "Who knows? He can't hold on to a steady job, so he moves around, stiffing landlords."

Matt had the impression that Lydia knew, but was deliberately being evasive. Knowing her, she probably wanted to be paid for the information. Didn't matter, he thought. It would be a simple enough thing for him to find out where his cousin was holed up these days. Scott would know. His older brother and Anthony had been fairly close all their lives. He knew for a fact that Scott's wife hated Anthony and thought of him as a bad influence, but that didn't stop Scott from getting together with his cousin.

It was time to get going. "Thanks for your time, Aunt Lydia."

"Sure." Standing in his way, she made no attempt to move. Instead, she looked at him expectantly. "Got a little sugar for your Aunt Lydia?"

Instead of kissing the old woman's cheek, the way Natalie assumed he was going to given the expression, she was surprised to see Matt digging into his pocket. Taking out his wallet, he handed the older woman several hundred dollar bills.

Lydia Silecchia beamed. Her satisfied, wide smile

seemed to create tiny fissures in the thick, caked-on foundation she wore, accenting her flaws rather than hiding them.

"You were always a good boy," Lydia said, quickly stuffing the bills into the folds of the flowing electric-blue caftan.

Natalie took in a deep, cleansing breath the moment they walked out of the stuffy apartment with its aging dust.

"As I remember it," she said to Matt as they went down the stairwell, "you were a bad boy, not a good one."

At the time, it seemed expedient to cultivate that kind of rebel persona. Beneath it all, he was always the same honorable guy. Even though that brought consequences with it.

"You do what you have to do in order to survive," he told her, then allowed himself a momentary smile. "Was that what attracted you to me? Because you had a thing for 'bad boys?'"

What had attracted her, she thought, was that she believed she saw the good heart beneath the rebel act. But she knew he'd deny it if she mentioned that.

"It had a certain appeal back then," she told him vaguely. He held the outer door for her. They didn't have far to go to reach his vehicle. She noticed that a couple of teens were wistfully eyeing the sports car.

Matt hit the security locks and they popped up in harmony. "And now?"

He knew the answer to that without her saying anything. She'd already given too much away by making love to him. She got in on her side of the car.

"Now we're on the trail of a killer," she said, her tone all business. The click of her seat belt as the metal met the groove underscored her words. "Do you think your cousin is capable of killing someone?"

He gave her question minimal thought. "Anthony has a short fuse and flies off the handle a lot, but as far as killing someone, no I don't think so. Anthony's always been just a lot of noise, no substance."

But everyone had their breaking point, she thought as they pulled away from the curb.

"Candace could drive people crazy. She rubbed more than a few people the wrong way," she recalled. "If he tried to steal the ring from her and she started to fight him off—"

Natalie didn't finish her sentence. Instead, she looked at Matt, waiting for either his firm denial or tacit agreement.

"Could have happened that way," he agreed with a thoughtful nod. "But she would have had to *really* tick him off. I want to talk to Anthony before I make up my mind one way or another."

That sounded reasonable. "Sure, let's go." Everything about her alert body language said she was ready to confront this cousin of his.

"Not this second," Matt informed her. "Aside from not knowing where he is at the moment, I've got to get back to The Janus and take care of a few more things before I go hunting for my cousin. Want me to drop you off at your house?"

What she wanted was to start hunting for Anthony immediately. But she knew that tone Matt was using. He would get to it when he could. There was no point in trying to argue him out of it.

So she shrugged her shoulders in a careless manner

and straightened in her seat to stare straight ahead. "Sure, my house is good."

Natalie had agreed a little too quickly, he thought. That wasn't good. "Promise me you're not going to go off on your own to see Anthony."

"How can I?" Natalie countered innocently. "I don't have his address, remember?"

He knew her too well. That wasn't enough to deter Natalie when she made up her mind about something. He wanted her word.

"Promise me," Matt insisted. "Or so help me, Nat, I'll tie you up and leave you in the trunk of my car until I can go with you."

He was probably perverse enough to make good on that, she thought. "Okay, okay, I promise." She saw Matt slant a skeptical glance at her as he drove through the green light. "What's the matter, Matt? Don't you trust me?"

No further than I can throw that great little butt of yours. "No," he said flatly, "not when it comes to things like this."

"I'll wait," she told him, making an *X* across her heart and holding up her hand in a solemn pledge. "As long as you promise that we'll go find him today."

"The minute I finish up at The Janus," he said. He saw her frustrated frown. "I do work for a living," he reminded her. "Okay, so it's settled? I'm taking you to your place?"

She changed her mind and shook her head. "No, drop me off at the police station. I want to see if I can get either Parker or Davidson to tell me if they've made any headway."

He remembered the disapproving look on the beefier detective's face when Parker saw that she was trying to view The Janus's security tapes. "I thought that you people aren't supposed to talk about a current investigation."

"Today was Candace's memorial service. I think that's enough for one of them to cut me a little slack in the territorial department."

Her answer made him laugh. "You know, Natalie, you're devious enough to be a Schaffer."

"Or a Rothchild." Natalie wasn't smiling as she said it.

"Touché," he replied.

Natalie stood in front of the police station steps and waved as Matt drove off. Turning, she walked slowly inside. But once within the building, she didn't go upstairs to the homicide division to touch base with either of the two detectives handling her sister's murder. Instead, she took the stairs down to the basement where the forensic lab was housed and the computer techs all did their work.

Her specific target was Silas Hunter, a highly skilled computer tech who had a crush on her. Barely twenty, the blond-haired Silas was far too young for her—even if she were inclined to date, which she wasn't—and she had gently told him so more than once.

However, she knew he still wanted to curry favor with her, and just this one time, because it was so important, she was going to let him ride to her rescue. The best part about Silas was that he was long on abilities and short on questions.

He brightened up the moment he saw her walking into his small section of the room. After exchanging a few pleasantries with him and accepting his condolences regarding her twin, Natalie took a blank piece of paper from his desk and wrote down Anthony Silecchia's name. She slid the paper in front of Silas.

"I need an address for this person," she told him.

Silas looked at the name, then raised his eyes to hers. "Fugitive or suspect?"

She didn't want to brand Silecchia yet. "Just someone who likes to stay one step ahead of the bill collectors," she said, plucking the first answer out of the air she could think of.

Silas laid the paper back down on his desk. "What was his last known address?"

"Don't know," she admitted.

Silas nodded his head as if that was a perfectly acceptable answer. His fingers began to race over the keyboard. Within seconds, he had Anthony Silecchia's likeness on the screen. He'd pulled up the man's driver's license.

"According to his Nevada license," Silas read, "he lives, or lived, on Galaxy Street." He tagged on the house number. "1589."

"Okay, that's a start," she said. He probably wasn't there any longer. Lydia had said he moved around. "Thanks."

"Hold it," Silas called after her, halting her retreat.

More furious typing and within seconds, Silas had pulled up an entire credit history complete with several more known residences, including a motel that wasn't too far away from the casino that her father owned.

And very close to the condo where Candace was killed, she realized. Natalie's fingertips turned icy.

Before she could ask him to, Silas had hit the print

button, and the printer beside his computer spit out two pages in rapid fire. He held them out to her. "Anything else?" he wanted to know.

Taking the pages, Natalie skimmed over them, and she shook her head. She couldn't have asked for more. The man had to be at one of these places. If he wasn't, then maybe someone there knew where he had gone.

"Nope. This'll do fine. You're a doll, Silas. I owe you." As she walked away, she heard the young tech sigh, as if he knew that the one thing he would have wanted, he couldn't have.

Walking toward the stairwell, Natalie went down the list of past addresses more slowly. From the looks of it, Anthony's residences had been taken up in progressively worse areas.

With the proceeds from the ring—if he *had* the ring—he could move back up in the world.

She could feel her scalp tingling as she studied the last address. Was he there? For how long? Maybe he was preparing to leave, even now.

A restlessness pervaded her.

Natalie knew that she'd promised Matt she wouldn't do anything or go looking for Anthony on her own. She knew she'd said she'd wait until he was free, but what if waiting cost her the opportunity to corner Silecchia?

She couldn't just stand around, killing time until Matt was free.

Besides, if this turned out to be a wild goose chase, she didn't want Matt wasting his time. He might grow impatient with the whole thing and tell her to leave it to the police.

At which point, she'd be on her own. Something she

normally was, but this one time, she had to admit she liked being partnered with him. Besides, it wasn't going to be for that long. He'd be gone soon enough.

At least that was the excuse she gave herself, the one that she decided would be acceptable to Matt if he called her out for going back on her word. She *wasn't* going back on it, she insisted silently. She was just bending it a little.

Besides, Matt knew her. He hadn't really expected her to do nothing, had he?

Natalie posed the rhetorical question to herself as she took a card out of her wallet. On it was the number of a local cab company. She needed to get to that motel quickly.

Twenty very long minutes later, the cab arrived. Another minute after that, she was on her way over to Anthony Silecchia's last known address, struggling to subdue her growing agitation.

The ride there took less time than waiting for the cab had.

"Want me to wait?" the cabbie asked as he brought his green-and-white vehicle to a stop at the curb. Beyond it was the motel. It appeared to be somewhat rundown, even from a distance.

"No, thanks." Getting out, she paid her fare. Natalie included a healthy tip because the cabbie hadn't droned endlessly on and on during the ride but had let her have her solitude.

Glancing at the money, the cabbie's thin lips parted in a smile.

"You sure?" he asked, sounding genuinely concerned as he glanced once more at the surrounding area. "This ain't the nicest neighborhood, Miss."

"I'll be all right," she assured him, stepping away from the cab.

She didn't have her usual second weapon strapped to the inside of her thigh because, after all, she'd attended a family funeral. But that didn't keep her from bringing along her personal small handgun, housing it in her clutch purse.

Natalie fervently hoped that she wouldn't have to use it.

Verifying Silecchia's room number with the bored-looking clerk behind the desk in the rental office, Natalie hurried up the outer stairs.

Room number 221 was in the middle of the second floor. It looked out onto the front parking lot.

She knocked on the door. There was no response, no sound of someone moving around inside. Waiting a moment, Natalie knocked again. Still nothing.

Dust-laden curtains hung at the window, drawn, but not meeting completely. She shifted so that she could see into the motel room. Squinting, she could make out the form of a man, his back to the window, sitting in a chair. His head looked as if it was dropped forward.

She realized that the man's hands were pulled back behind him. They were tied. Something was very definitely up.

"Time to make an entrance," she murmured, reaching into her purse for her weapon. She tried knocking one last time. This time, there was a frantic noise from within the room. As she peered in, she realized that Anthony Silecchia had twisted around and was looking straight at her. There was desperation in his eyes as he frantically tugged on the ties on his wrists.

Natalie quickly studied the door. She judged that it wasn't that sturdy. Backing up, she raised her leg and kicked the door as hard as she could. The wood groaned but ultimately stayed where it was.

She tried again. It took Natalie three very strong kicks before the door surrendered, separating itself from the doorjamb.

One forceful shove from her shoulder was all that was necessary. Natalie quickly let herself in.

"Anthony Silecchia I presume?" she quipped, crossing to the man in the chair.

Tucking the handgun she'd had out just a moment before into her waistband, she started to loosen the man's ties. Or attempted to.

That was when she heard it. The very distinctive click of a gun being cocked.

At the same time she heard a husky, whiskey-lubricated voice order, "Drop it."

She knew that voice.

Stunned, Natalie turned around.

"I said drop it!" Lydia shouted at her. She appeared to be less than half a step away from being enraged. "And while you're at it, raise your hands up over your head." When Natalie didn't obey, Lydia gestured with the gun she was holding. "Now," she growled.

For the time being, Natalie played along and did as she was told. "I thought you said you didn't know where he was."

"I got lucky," Lydia snapped impatiently. "And this is none of your damn business. I know who you are," she shouted angrily. "You're that blond tart's sister. Thought you fooled me, didn't you?" she accused.

There'd been no attempt at any deception. "Matt told you my name when we first came over," Natalie reminded the woman.

Lydia didn't appear to remember, or if she did, she gave no indication. Instead, the bloodshot hazel eyes shifted over to the nephew she'd caught off guard and tied up.

"I want that ring back, Anthony. Do you hear me?" She cocked the trigger. "I want it back. It belongs to me!"

Anthony looked at his aunt as if she was insane. "I don't have any damn ring, you crazy old hag."

"Not any damn ring," Lydia shouted into his face. "*The* damn ring. The Tears of the Quetzal. It's mine," she screamed at him. "I *earned* it. I was nice to that horrible bastard with the cold hands. *Real* nice," she emphasized.

Natalie felt nauseous. The thought of Lydia and her father together made her stomach turn and threatened to bring up her hastily consumed lunch.

"The ring doesn't belong to you," Natalie told Lydia as calmly as possible. The calmer she sounded, the more agitated Lydia became.

"The hell it doesn't. What doesn't belong in this picture is you. You stumbled into the wrong damn place this time, girlie. I'm going to get rid of you as soon as Anthony tells me where the ring is." A nasty, cold smile curved her thin, cracked lips. "Maybe even before. That'll teach you not to stick your nose where it doesn't belong."

As she spoke, she shifted the small gun barrel so that it could deliver a nice sized hole to whatever area she chose.

Chapter 15

Natalie raised her hands as she was told and kept a watchful eye on the gun in Lydia's hand.

"You don't want to do this," she said to the woman.

Something almost maniacal flashed in Lydia's eyes. "Oh, yes I do."

She meant it, Natalie thought. The woman really was crazy. "Did you kill Candace?" she asked Lydia bluntly.

Lydia cocked her head as if that could make her think better. She reminded Natalie of an aging bird.

"If I had, I'd have the ring, wouldn't I? No, *he* killed her. Anthony," Lydia declared, momentarily shifting both her line of vision and her weapon, pointing both at her nephew.

Taking advantage of the woman's momentary distraction, Natalie moved to grab her.

But Lydia was surprisingly agile for a woman in her deranged state.

"Uh-uh-uh," she cautioned in a singsong voice. "I wouldn't do that if I were you." The red lips parted in a cold smile. "Not unless you want to die a few minutes earlier."

Natalie was aware that the disheveled, bedraggled Anthony was frantically tugging on the ropes around his wrists—and getting nowhere.

"Aunt Lydia, get these damn ropes off me and stop talking crazy. I don't have the freakin' ring, and I didn't kill that woman. When I got there, she was already dead. And the ring was gone," he insisted.

Natalie could just picture Matt's cousin ready to eagerly pull the diamond off her sister's dead hand. She stifled her rage. That wouldn't help her get out of this situation.

"I got the hell out of there," he swore, pleading with his aunt.

"Do you drive a navy-blue sedan?" Natalie asked suddenly. Just yesterday, a woman had called in on the tip line. She'd said that she was walking her dog in the vicinity of Candace's condo around midnight the night she died and had seen a navy-blue sedan peeling away.

Confusion mingled with fear in his eyes. "Yeah, what about it?" Anthony whined.

"She's looking for her sister's killer, that's 'what about it,'" Lydia taunted, talking to him as if she were the one with superior intelligence. "She doesn't care who she pins it on, as long as somebody pays. Your cousin Matt brought her sniffing around." When Lydia frowned, her mouth pointed downward. "Never did like him."

The woman was incredible, Natalie thought in disgust.

She remembered what Lydia had said when Matt handed her the hundred-dollar bills. "But you took his money."

Lydia tossed her head proudly. "I *always* take the money." And then her expression changed, her eyes narrowing into slits. "Okay, I'm getting bored. This is where you check out. And don't worry, I won't miss. The only thing my worthless husband taught me was how to shoot and get what I aimed for."

Just as Lydia was about to squeeze the trigger, the door banged open for a second time in less than fifteen minutes. It crashed against the opposite wall. Startled, Lydia jerked her head around to see who was behind her.

It was all that Natalie needed.

She lunged at Lydia, tucking her head down and aiming for the woman's hips. They both fell to the stained, tattered carpet. With a death grip on her weapon, Lydia's finger jerked, firing the gun. Behind her, Natalie heard Anthony scream. She didn't get a chance to look up to see who had come in until, straddling Lydia, she pinned down the woman's toothpick-thin arms.

"Matt," she cried, relief flooding through her. "And you brought reinforcements." Natalie's smile went from ear to ear. "Nice to see you."

"You, too," he wisecracked, in order to hide the swell of emotion he was feeling. If he'd been half a minute later, she might not have even been alive. He felt like strangling Lydia with his bare hands. But instead, he stepped aside and let the two policemen he'd brought with him take over.

"I'm bleeding to death!" Anthony all but shrieked. "Help me, Matt!

Matt took Natalie's hand and helped her up to her feet. He glanced toward his cousin. It looked as if the bullet had hardly grazed him. There was a bullet hole in the wall right behind him.

"It's a flesh wound, Tony. Suck it up." One of the policemen untied Anthony while the other led Lydia away. She was cursing at everything in sight, most venomously at him. Matt completely ignored the woman. His attention was focused on Natalie. "And as for you—" He didn't know whether to hug her because she was alive or shake her because she could have been killed. So he just held onto her shoulders for a moment, exhaling a rather loud breath. "I knew I couldn't trust you."

He had to understand. "It's not a matter of trust. I just wanted to spare you some unnecessary work. In case you haven't noticed, your Aunt Lydia is a loon," she said, looking as the woman was being led out the door, "and she could have made the whole thing up. I just wanted to make sure she hadn't."

And then the circumstances suddenly dawned on her. How had he managed to come in the nick of time? "I thought you said you didn't know where Anthony was staying."

"I didn't," he confirmed. "But I figured my brother Scott would, so I gave him a call." He looked at her, his eyes saying volumes. "Lucky for you I did." *And lucky for me*, he added silently.

Natalie saw no reason to dispute that. "Lucky," she echoed, walking out. Both Anthony and Lydia were being placed in the backseat of the police car. Within seconds, they would be on their way to the police precinct.

"Find out anything?" Matt asked her, bringing her attention back to him.

Turning her head, she realized that they were less than a couple of inches apart—and she had this overwhelming desire just to lay her head on his shoulder. "Anthony admits to being at my sister's condo. According to him, she was already dead."

"You believe him?" Matt asked. He was inclined to. His cousin was a lot of things, most of them unsavory, but he sincerely doubted that the man was a killer. He was too much of a coward for that.

Natalie shrugged, not sure what to believe. "We had a tip from a dog walker who saw someone driving a car like Anthony's away from the scene about midnight. The ME thinks Candace was killed before then." She looked at the departing police vehicle. "Frankly, right now, my money's on your aunt. She's crazy enough to have done it and spacey enough not to remember doing it." She looked back at Matt. "I want to be there when they question her."

He had no doubt that she would get her way, even though this still wasn't supposed to be her case. "I'm sure you'll pull it off."

Natalie nodded. Suddenly, she felt as if her facade was crumbling. She looked up at the man beside her. "Thanks for not trusting me and coming to the rescue."

He grinned, for the moment forgetting the agitation he'd experienced when he couldn't reach her on her cell phone.

"Anytime." And then he grew serious. His eyes swept over her as if to reassure himself. "Did she hurt you?"

Natalie shrugged. "I'll probably have some bruises.

She's a very bony old lady, but no, she didn't." She took a deep breath, as if to fortify herself. "Could have been a lot worse if you hadn't shown up."

He laughed shortly, draping one arm protectively around her shoulders. Grateful that he'd acted on impulse.

"It was the funniest thing. Right in the middle of going over the revised expense report for the new surveillance equipment, I had the oddest feeling suddenly come over me. A premonition I guess. I had this very clear image of you—and you were in trouble. I just 'sensed' it." His voice had a mocking quality to it because he was the type who usually didn't believe in those kinds of things.

"Maybe you're taking Candace's place," Natalie theorized. "When Candace and I were younger, I swear each of us knew when the other was in trouble or even needed the other. When we grew up, that didn't happen so much. I think we were both just blocking that sixth sense out." Her expression grew very serious. "But the night Candace was killed, I had this horrible, icy sensation slice right through me. I was just falling asleep, and I bolted upright."

She shrugged. "But I thought I was just having a nightmare, so I let it go. Maybe it wasn't a nightmare. Maybe it was Candace, trying to reach out to me one last time for help."

Matt didn't try to argue her out of it. Neither did he agree outright. There were things in this world, he had come to know, that just defied logic and straightforward explanations. Like his suddenly feeling that she'd needed him.

"Maybe," he finally echoed. He looked around the motel parking lot. "Where's your car?"

"I took a cab from the police station. I didn't want to waste time going home to get my car," she explained. "I was afraid that maybe, if he *had* killed Candace, your cousin would bolt."

Matt nodded. In her place, he would have thought the same thing. "Worked a little magic on the computer to get the address?"

Her smile struck him as almost shy. Something stirred within him, and he recognized it for what it was. Not just yearning, but deep affection. "More like worked a little magic on the computer tech."

"Poor guy probably couldn't say no to you." A fond smile curved his mouth. "I know the feeling."

She thought of the letter she found beneath his pillow that awful morning. "As I recall, you said no in your own way."

He made no comment. Instead, he asked her, "Need a ride?"

She was feeling suddenly very vulnerable around Matt, but it would take time to get a cab to come and pick her up. "Yeah."

Matt opened the passenger door for her and waited until she got in.

They went to the police station where Natalie filled in an annoyed Detective Parker on the latest details regarding her sister's case. In exchange for this information, Parker grudgingly allowed her to sit in on the interviews. Anthony held fast to his story that he had nothing to do with Candace's murder, that she was already dead when he got there.

Lydia, however, rambled on and on. Finding holes in

her story and discovering that she believed the ring really belonged to her, the detectives began to believe that she had been the one to end Candace's life. When Parker finally confronted her and asked if she shoved Candace, causing the heiress to fall backward and hit her head on the marble coffee table, Lydia merely shrugged and said "Maybe."

Lydia was booked for Candace's murder within the hour.

"But then where's the ring?" Matt voiced the question out loud that was on both their minds.

Upon leaving the precinct, he'd brought Natalie back with him to The Janus. He needed to pick up his wallet, he told her, explaining that when he couldn't reach her on her cell phone, he'd left in a hurry, inadvertently leaving his wallet in his desk. He wanted to get it before he filled her in on his agenda.

Following Matt to his office, Natalie shrugged. "Who knows? She might have it, or she could have lost it, along with her mind. As far as I'm concerned, if the ring is lost, well, good riddance. It's brought my family nothing but bad luck."

Opening the middle drawer of his desk, Matt took out his wallet and tucked it into his pocket.

"Maybe not." He took her arm and gently guided her back out again. "In an odd sort of way, it brought you and me together."

She was very aware that he was touching her and drew away. She might as well start getting used to the separation. "But for how long?"

They were out on the casino floor now and perforce,

he had to get closer in order for her to hear him above the din. "That depends."

She felt his breath along her neck and throat. Not a good thing when she was trying to harden herself. "On what?"

"On how long you'll have me."

Those were the last words she expected to hear. Natalie came to a dead stop and looked at him. "Have you for what?"

"For anything you want." He took her hands in his. "I can't begin to tell you what it did to me when I thought something had happened to you." It was time to stop playing it safe, he told himself. Time for admission because life could be very short and what he had with Natalie was rare. He'd been a fool to walk away from it, even for the best of reasons. "I never stopped loving you, Natalie."

"Then why did you disappear like that?" she wanted to know. "An occasional card on Christmas would have been nice."

The only defense he had was the truth. "I left for your own good. It wasn't for mine." However, that was in the past, and he was going to find a way to make this work, no matter what. "But I realized that I really can't make it without you."

He watched her face, afraid of what her answer might be. Matt was incredibly relieved to see her smile. "Took you long enough."

Thank you, God. I owe you one, he thought. "Some of us are slow learners."

She bit her tongue to keep from making a comment. Instead, she asked, "Now what?"

This was where his agenda came in. He'd already

made plans. "Now I'm going to take a few weeks off and show you a good time. And then, after we get back, you can decide if you want to marry me."

It took everything she had not to let her mouth drop open. But she managed. "I already made that decision," she told him. "Eight years ago."

Oh damn, how did one man get to be so lucky, he wondered. There was another side to the legend of the ring, he recalled. That in the right hands, it brought true love almost immediately. Neither one of them had laid their hands on the ring, but it was as if it was still working its magic.

"And you haven't changed your mind?" he asked her.

She shook her head. "Not even when I wanted to fillet you. Idiot," she declared, lacing her arms around his neck. "I gave my heart away once—and it never came back." She sighed, as if resigned. "You still have it."

His arms closed around her. "Nice to know," he told her.

He was watching the Rothchild woman from across the casino floor. She had a lot more class than her twin'd had, but that wasn't going to save her. Class or breeding, or whatever the hell they wanted to call it, wasn't going to save any of them.

They were all living on borrowed time.

He was going to bide his time and take them out, one by one, the way he'd promised he would in his note to the old man.

Sins of the fathers, he thought, feeling righteous. They couldn't avoid their fate.

But for now, Patrick Moore was going to enjoy himself by getting under her skin like the media reporter he was pretending to be. Unlike Candace, he knew that Natalie Rothchild hated publicity and shunned it. She just wanted to live her life like an ordinary woman.

But she wasn't an ordinary woman. She was a Rothchild, and all the Rothchilds had to pay for what they'd done to his father. To his mother. And thus, to him.

Coming to life just as he saw the Rothchild woman kiss her companion, Patrick elbowed and pushed his way through the crowd. As he did, he raised his voice, calling out her name, doing his best to ruin her moment and get people to look in her direction.

"Hey, Natalie! Detective Rothchild! Word's out that they caught your sister's killer. What do you have to say about that? Think they've got the right person, or is he or she still out there, waiting to get another one of you?"

He got a kick out of asking, out of taunting her. It was doubly delicious because he knew the deranged old woman hadn't killed Candace.

He had.

Not on purpose, but by accident. But hell, that accident felt damn good when he realized she was dead. One look at her face had told him Candace Rothchild had posed for her last picture.

As he drew closer to his target, Patrick held a press card over his head to identify himself. It was like a brazen shield that indicated he had every right to bombard her with invasive questions. He knew it infuriated her.

Shoving people out of the way, he was intent on getting right up into Natalie's face, and the crowd was making that almost impossible. Getting into her face was part of his plan. He'd already done it twice to her father. He intended to do it to all of them, to make all their lives as miserable as possible—just before he ended them.

"Damn it, get out of my way," he cursed, punching the heavyset man in front of him in the kidneys.

Rather than doubling up, the man swung around and punched him in the face. Ten feet short of Natalie, Patrick Moore found himself entangled in a fistfight with a beefy stranger who was growling curses at him.

Patrick had always had a short fuse, and it had only gotten shorter with time. It took very little to unleash his maniacal side. He swung back, trading blows with the stranger. The man clearly outweighed him, but Patrick had been raised on the street. As a street fighter, he knew every dirty move there was.

Blessed with antennae when it came to his own survival, above the stranger's cursing and the crowd cheering them on, Patrick heard the man with Rothchild calling for security. The next second, the guy came running over to break up the fight himself.

Security would call the police!

The thought telegraphed itself through his brain, ushering in a sense of panic. He wasn't afraid of the police, or being in jail. Hell, he could do time standing on his head. But he couldn't afford to have the police frisk him. They'd find the ring in his pocket.

Damn it, what was he going to do now?

Out of the corner of his eye, as Patrick ducked out of the way of another punch and gauged that his opponent's arms were getting too heavy for him to keep swinging them like that, he saw a tall, willowy blonde in a body-clinging red minidress. She was almost tottering from side to side in her stiletto heels. The blonde looked a little spooked and definitely out of her element.

An out-of-towner, he thought. Even so, there was something about her that set her apart. Patrick was confident that he'd be able to pick her out of a crowd if he had to.

Besides, he didn't have much of a choice.

Swinging around, he deliberately brought the fight into her area, knocking the other guy into her. The oversized purse she was hanging on to as if her very life depended on it went crashing to the ground. Its contents came flying out.

In the middle of the fight, Patrick flung an apology her way, grabbing up the purse and holding it out to her before the other man hit him again. What neither she, his flagging opponent nor the crowd that had gathered around them seemed to notice was that Patrick Moore swiftly transferred the Tears of the Quetzal from his pocket into the depths of the cavernous purse.

"Break it up!" Matt shouted, ramming his shoulder between the two men. "You boys want to go down to the precinct to cool off?"

"Hell, he started it," the offended stranger complained, gasping for breath. "I was just trying to get back to the slot machines."

"Sorry, man. Lost my head," Patrick mumbled, nursing his cut lip. "If I don't get in a good story by the end of the day, my editor's going to fire me. I got a family to feed."

The other man looked instantly sympathetic. But Matt didn't.

"Well, you're not getting a story here," Matt informed

him, moving so that his body actually blocked the man's access to Natalie.

Patrick held up his hands, as if surrendering. Right now, it was important to just be able to slip away. There was time enough to get back to the Rothchild bitch. She wasn't going anywhere.

"Okay, okay, sorry. Won't happen again," he promised, backpedaling.

"See that it doesn't." Matt turned back to Natalie, already forgetting the incident. Having the pair arrested would mean more paperwork, and he had something better to do. He had a date with a beautiful lady and a lot of lost time to make up for.

Seeming to rub his cut lip, Patrick hid his smile behind his hand and then looked around.

The smile vanished.

As had the woman with the oversized purse.

* * * * *

Celebrate 60 years of pure reading pleasure with Harlequin®!

Step back in time and enjoy a sneak preview of an exciting anthology from Harlequin® Historical with **THE DIAMONDS OF WELBOURNE MANOR**

This compelling anthology features three stories about the outrageous Fitzmanning sisters. Meet Annalise, who is never at a loss for words… But that can change with an unexpected encounter in the forest.

Available May 2009 from Harlequin® Historical.

"I'm the illegitimate daughter of notoriously scandalous parents, Mr. Milford. Candidates for my hand are unlikely to be lining up at the gates."

"Don't be so quick to discount your charms, my dear. Or the charm of your substantial dowry. Or even your brothers' influence. There are as many reasons to marry as there are marriages."

Annalise snorted. "Oh, yes. Perhaps I shall marry for dynastic reasons, or perhaps for property or influence. After all, a loveless, practical marriage worked out so well for my mother."

"Well, you've routed me on that one. I can think of no suitable rejoinder." Ned rose to his feet and extended his hand. "And since that is the case, let me be the first to wish you a long and happy spinsterhood."

Her mouth gaped open. And then she laughed.

And he froze.

This was the first time, Ned realized. The first time he'd seen her eyes light up and her mouth curl. The first time he'd witnessed her features melded together in glorious accord to produce exquisite beauty.

Unbelievable what a change came over her face. Unheard of what effect her throaty, rasping laughter had on his body. It pounded a beat upon his ear, quickly taken up by his pulse. It echoed through him, finally residing in his stirring nether regions.

So easily she did it, awakened these sensations within him—without any apparent effort at all. And she had called him potentially dangerous? Clearly the intelligent thing for him to do would be to steer clear, to leave her to the tender ministrations of Lord Peter Blackthorne.

"You were right." She smiled up at him as she took his hand and climbed to her feet. "I do feel better."

Ah, well. When had he ever chosen the intelligent path?

He did not relinquish her hand. He used it to pull her in, close enough that he could feel the warmth of her. "At the risk of repeating Lord Peter's mistake and anticipating too much—may I ask if you'll be my partner in battledore tomorrow?"

Her smile dimmed. Her breath came a little faster. His own had gone shallow, as if he'd just run a race—and lost. He ran his gaze over the appealing lift of her brow and the curious angle of her chin. His index finger twitched.

"I should like that," she said.

His finger trembled again and he lifted it, traced the pink and tender shell of her ear, the unique sweep of her jaw. Her pulse leaped beneath her skin, triggering his own. Slowly he tilted her chin up, waiting for her to object, to step back, to slap his hand away.

She did none of those eminently sensible things. Which left him free to do the entirely impractical thing.

Baby soft, the skin of her lips. Her whole body trembled when he touched her there.

He leaned in. Her eyes closed, even as she stood straight against him, strung as tight as a bow. He pressed his mouth to hers. It was a soft kiss, sweet and chaste. And yet he was hot and hard and as ready as he'd ever been in his life.

She drew back a little. Sighed. Their breath mingled a moment before she slowly backed away.

"Oh," she breathed. Her dark eyes were full of wonder and something that looked like fear. He took a step toward her, but she only shook her head. His outstretched hand fell to his side as she turned to disappear into the wood. This was the first time, Ned realized. The first time, since he'd come to the house party at Welbourne Manor, that he'd seen her eyes light up.

* * * * *

Follow Ned and Annalise's story in May 2009 in
THE DIAMONDS OF WELBOURNE MANOR
Available May 2009 from Harlequin® Historical.

Available in the series romance section,
or in the historical romance section,
wherever books are sold.

**We'll be spotlighting a different series
every month throughout 2009
to celebrate our 60th anniversary.**

Look for Harlequin® Historical in May!

**60 years of Harlequin,
600 years of romance
in Harlequin Historical!**

www.eHarlequin.com   HHBPA09

REQUEST YOUR FREE BOOKS!

2 FREE NOVELS PLUS 2 FREE GIFTS!

Sparked by Danger, Fueled by Passion!

SRS09

You're invited to join our Tell Harlequin Reader Panel!

By joining our new reader panel you will:

- Receive Harlequin® books—they are FREE and yours to keep with no obligation to purchase anything!
- Participate in fun online surveys
- Exchange opinions and ideas with women just like you
- Have a say in our new book ideas and help us publish the best in women's fiction

In addition, you will have a chance to win great prizes and receive special gifts! See Web site for details. Some conditions apply. Space is limited.

To join, visit us at
www.TellHarlequin.com.

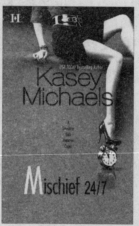

Silhouette®

Romantic

SUSPENSE

COMING NEXT MONTH

Available April 28, 2009

#1559 LADY KILLER—Kathleen Creighton
The Taken
When Tony Whitehall is enlisted to find out more about
Brooke Fallon Grant, who's accused of murdering her abusive ex-husband,
she insists that she—and her pet cougar, Lady—are
innocent. Sparks fly between Tony and Brooke as they try to save
the animal's life and discover who the killer really is.

#1560 HIS 7-DAY FIANCÉE—Gail Barrett
Love in 60 Seconds
Starting a new life in Las Vegas, Amanda Patterson never predicted she'd
be assaulted by a gunman in a casino. Owner Luke Montgomery fears bad
publicity and convinces her to keep quiet. When someone tries to kidnap
her daughter, Amanda agrees to Luke's plan to temporarily move in with
him and act as his fiancée, but their growing attraction soon puts them all
in danger.

#1561 NIGHT RESCUER—Cindy Dees
H.O.T. Watch
Wracked with survivor's guilt, former Special Forces agent
John Hollister agrees to put his suicide on hold to deliver medical
researcher Melina Montez to the mountains of Peru. As sexual heat and
desire flare, she reveals the fatal mission she's on to rescue her family,
and together they challenge each other to fight to stay alive for love.

#1562 HIGH-STAKES HOMECOMING—Suzanne McMinn
Haven
Intending to lay claim to his inherited family farm, Penn Ramsey is
shocked to discover the woman who once broke his heart. Willa also
claims the farm is hers, and when a storm strands them at the house
together, they discover their attraction hasn't died and all isn't as it seems.
Is the house trying to keep them from leaving? Or is something—or
someone—else at work here?